# KEEPING LILY

A DARK ROMANCE

IZZY SWEET
SEAN MORIARTY

Copyright © 2016 by Izzy Sweet and Sean Moriarty
All rights reserved. This book or any portion thereof may not be reproduced
or used in any manner whatsoever without the express written permission of
the publisher except for the use of brief quotations in a book review.
Published by Izzy Sweet and Sean Moriarty

This is a work of fiction. Names, characters, businesses, places, events and
incidents are either the products of the author's imagination or used in a
fictitious manner. Any resemblance to actual persons, living or dead, or
actual events is purely coincidental.
Copyright © 2016 Izzy Sweet & Sean Moriarty

 Created with Vellum

## 1

LUCIFER

"*M*otherfucker!" Comes out of my mouth in a growl as I shake my hand.

The punch to this piece of shit's jaw sent tingling sensations up my arm.

Mickey Dalton sputters gibberish out of his busted lips. "I... I... Swear I will pay... just gotta..."

I'm tempted to keep this up, but fuck it. I have bigger fish to fry than this small time fucking gambler.

Looking over the man's shoulder, I nod to Andrew. "Ensure he fully understands how much he owes. Remove his pinky."

"Yes, sir." Andrew nods.

"Wha... No!" Mickey shouts as Andrew heads to the table where he keeps a black bag stowed.

Turning around, I look at Simon, my right-hand man. "Where are we at with the other three files?"

"Two have been collected on, the last I was waiting on your judgment."

"Marshall Dawson."

"He has flat out refused to cooperate with any of our attempts to collect. He believes his status is untouchable. He will give us no answer on where he was or what has happened to our money."

"Is he finally home?" I ask.

"Arrived earlier tonight."

A metallic snip rings out into the room followed by a high-pitched scream. I turn to see Andrew wiping the blood on the guy's t-shirt.

Andrew raises his voice only slightly as he grabs the man by the throat. "Stop fucking squealing, asshole. Lucifer doesn't like hearing pigs fucking about."

Walking out through the door and into the hall, I look to Simon. "How are the spreadsheets with Bart coming along?"

"Clean, with everything accounted for…"

"Yet, you still have doubts?" I ask him as we walk.

"I do. I just can't explain why."

"Keep an eye on him then."

∽

SIMON HOLDS an umbrella over my head as we walk out of the abandoned hotel. The shattered glass door slams shut behind us as he ushers me into the sleek black Mercedes SUV.

Getting comfortable in the backseat, I reach over and pull the file left on the other seat for me. The name Marshall Dawson is neatly typed on the tab.

I let out a quiet sigh to myself. I knew this one was going to come back as a thorn in my side.

Marshall Dawson is a waste of breathable air. The man used the connections he had with my father and another city boss to secure a loan from us. Five million in *cash*.

Five fucking million dollars with nothing to show for it.

Five fucking million dollars down the drain.

I took this on as a favor to Sean O'Riley. A favor to a now dead and buried man.

Shit like that doesn't sit well with me. But when I went to the top to seek retribution, I was stonewalled. I was told the man who killed Sean, and all the surrounding issues, have been dealt with.

Fuck that. I want my pound of flesh.

Shaking my head, I open the file. It's no use going down that train of thought right now. I can pursue it another time if I need to.

I slowly flip through the pages we have on Marshall.

It's funny how we can put a file together on a person where he is reduced to twenty or so pages. I can see every payment he has made on his mortgage to how many times he has been in the overdraft with his bank.

I look at his legal outstanding debts, and I look at the five-million-dollar debt he now owes to me personally. Anger is slowly creeping through my veins.

Flipping through the pages, I look at his family life. Since he borrowed the money I have had one of my men keeping close tabs on his family. He is married to Lilith Merriweather, aged twenty-seven, and has two children, a boy and a girl. Both children under the age of seven.

I look at the picture of Marshall for a long time as we drive through the late-night rain. The man is closer to my father's age than mine. How did he marry a woman so young? Money and his slimy charm must have played a large part of it.

I look through the pictures of his family quickly. The children are pretty in a child way. Blonde hair and blue eyes, they must take after their mother. Marshall must have married way out of his league.

My fingers stop as the picture of his wife comes up. Emerald green eyes, sensuous pink lips, high cheekbones, pale flawless skin and long blonde hair. All of those parts on their own would make her remarkable. Even if her face was overall plain just one of her features would stun a person. But together they make something otherworldly.

She is beauty incarnate.

Fingers tracing the lines of her lips, I frown. How the hell did that man marry a woman like this? I flip further through the pictures of her. There aren't many, but what I do see shows me that she is unlike any other woman I have ever laid eyes on.

She is perfection.

There is a rather candid photo of her putting groceries in the back of her red Volvo station wagon. Her hair is all over the place. Her slender legs are encased in yoga pants, feet in Uggs. Her daughter looks like she is giving her problems as she tries to watch her and still put groceries in the back.

Even this… domesticity calls to me.

There is a glamour shot of some type mixed in and I can see just how haunting those eyes are. They are calling to me, pulling me in to get forever lost. I can feel my hands curling into themselves. She is pulling me from where I sit in the SUV.

"Take me to Marshall's, James," I say to my driver.

Looking back at me from the front seat, Simon says, "Now? You don't want to wait until tomorrow?"

"No. We're going there *now*."

The car makes a few turns as we pull off the freeway and then back on again.

My eyes drift out the window for a moment to look at the rain that has been pelting down on the city all week.

Looking back to the picture, though, I see something I haven't seen before—a light. Inside I feel an ember flaring to life.

My muscles are going taut with expectation.

I need to see this woman; I need to see if what the pictures show me is true.

LILY

My husband, Marshall, is sleeping beside me, snoring loudly, and I have the strongest urge to smack him.

I want to scream in his pale, pudgy face. I want to tell him to wake the fuck up. I want to ask him why he's back in my bed.

But I just lay beside him and stare up at the ceiling instead.

It's time to accept reality.

Our marriage is done.

Dead.

Today was the final nail in the coffin.

First thing in the morning, after I get the kids off to school, I'm going to meet with a divorce attorney. I can't go on like this. This is no way to live, this is just...existing.

And I'm sick of it.

After growing up dirt poor, I married Marshall thinking I would finally have financial security. I would always have a roof over my head. I would never go hungry again.

Foolishly, I believed his lust for me would turn to love. That like an arranged marriage, our feelings for each other would grow after time. If we had children, we could make a real go of it.

But this, the lack of love, the lack of care, isn't worth it. I rather starve than stay in this loveless marriage.

Marshall has been gone for weeks, *traveling on business*. He's gone more than he's home. Ever since our first child, Adam, was born six years ago, he's been finding more and more reasons to leave us.

There's always some client on the other coast that needs his help. Or some corporation up north that has to have his expertise or they're going to lose millions on… something…

It's funny, even after almost eight years of marriage I still don't know exactly what his job title or true profession is. Whenever I ask him about it he just brushes me off, doesn't have time to explain it, or says I wouldn't understand.

Like I'm some kind of idiot.

If I was an idiot I wouldn't know about all the women he's been hooking up with. I know that's one of the reasons he's always leaving us. He has a girlfriend in every city.

Yet, he won't even touch me when I throw myself at him.

I sigh, looking down at the red nightie I bought from Victoria's Secret and pull the blanket up to cover my breasts.

He won't even touch me when I've taken great pains to dress up for him.

Suddenly my eyes feel swollen and my nose stings. I have to blink back my tears and take a deep breath. Rolling my eyes back up, I focus on the ceiling.

This shouldn't hurt, dammit. This isn't a bad thing, this is good.

This is… *freedom*.

I no longer have to pretend this is a real marriage. No more keeping up appearances on Facebook. No more making excuses for him with my family and friends.

No more trying to explain to the children that daddy is sorry but he had to miss their birthday—again.

This is a fresh start, a new beginning.

I've been doing everything on my own for years now. Losing him won't make much of a difference.

Marshall suddenly grunts loudly and rolls over.

The air turns sour and I resist the urge to gag.

*Gah, he is such a pig.*

## 2

LILY

I'm not sure what wakes me up. It could have been the light turning on.

Marshall's loud, "What the fuck?"

Or the soft, menacing voice that says, "Hello, Marshall. I'm not interrupting anything, am I?"

Even under my warm blanket, that voice sends a chill down my spine and I peel my eyes open, shivering.

At first, the light is too harsh on my eyes and I have to blink several times before the strange man standing in our bedroom comes into focus.

This must be a dream, I convince myself and squeeze my eyes shut. I open them again but I still just can't believe it.

There's no way that man is real.

Standing in the center of my bedroom, the man is illuminated by a halo of light coming from the lamp. The light seems to love him, clinging to him. He's glowing and so alluring, he looks almost angelic.

"What the fuck are you doing in my house? You can't just come walking in here…" Marshall sputters. His fat fists grab the blanket, yanking it away from me as he pulls it up his hairy chest.

I gasp as the cool air hits my breasts and the sound draws the attention of the angelic stranger. He turns his icy blue gaze on me and I'm utterly stunned as our eyes meet.

With just a look I feel held by him.

Trapped.

Frozen.

Helpless.

He's so beautiful it *hurts* to look upon him. The kind of beauty that's so strong, so deeply felt, it's like experiencing a piece of music that *moves* you and staring into the sun at the same time.

Tears prick my eyes and my skin tingles as I break out in gooseflesh.

His face is a composition of features so perfect that now that I've glimpsed them I fear all other men will be forever compared to him.

Chiseled cheeks, full, pink lips. A strong jaw and straight nose. Blonde hair so pale it's nearly snow white and brushed back from his forehead.

It feels like an eternity passes as we stare at each other across my bedroom and then his eyes break away only to slide down, warming as they lock on the pale swells of my breasts.

A flush creeps up my chest. I'm not naked but in this little lacy nightie, I feel like I am.

I grab the blanket and Marshall cries out as I yank it back. He shoots me a dirty look but I give him my coldest glare and practically dare him to try and take it back.

Screw him, no one cares about his hairy man-chest.

The stranger watches our little tug of war, his lips curving with a hint of amusement.

Marshall finally gives up on trying to wrestle the blanket away from me and decides to steal my pillow instead. Covering his chest with my pillow, he hugs it tightly and puffs up as he says, "If you leave now, Lucifer, I'll forget this incident ever happened."

Lucifer? Is that the stranger's name? How strange and morbid. Yet, I swear I've heard that name before, on the news or in the paper...

The stranger's eyes flash and the amusement disappears from his lips. Two dark shadows shimmer behind him and I swallow back a gasp as I realize those two shadows are two other men.

What the hell is going on? Who are these men and why are they in my bedroom? I turn to Marshall and watch him squirm uneasily.

What did Marshall do?

"You'll forget this ever happened?" Lucifer says coolly and his eyes narrow with menace. "Just like you forgot to pay me back the five million dollars you owe me?"

All the color drains instantly from Marshall's face and his eyes dart from side to side as if he's trying to figure out an escape plan. "I already paid that back. You'll have to talk to Sean if you want your money."

"Sean's dead."

I watch Marshall's mouth open then close, then open again. He sputters and gasps like a fish out of water, his face starting to turn blue from the lack of oxygen.

I can't believe Marshall borrowed five million dollars. What would he need with so much money? I know I haven't seen a penny of it.

"I paid Sean the money," Marshall finally gets out, and then rushes on to say, "I don't have five million to pay you..."

Lucifer takes a step towards our bed. "That's too bad."

"Wait!" Marshall cries out in panic, the grip of his fingers tearing at the pillow he holds to his chest. "Maybe we can work something out? I could—"

"I've had a look at your assets. You have no means to pay me back," Lucifer says dismissively and takes another step toward the bed.

I look between Lucifer and Marshall and now I'm starting to feel panicked. Lucifer has only taken two steps towards our bed but there's clear menace in the way he's moving.

What is he going to do? Are they going to hurt Marshall?

Are they going to hurt me?

Lucifer takes another step and Marshall whimpers. He *whimpers.*

The sound has my hackles rising and I wonder if there's something I could do. I glance towards my phone on my nightstand. The moment I don't think they're looking at me I'm going to make a grab for it.

But it might be too late for Marshall by then…

I could start screaming, but the only good that will probably do is wake the children.

Marshall is pushing back against the headboard like he believes he could escape through the wall if he tries hard enough. Then he shoots a pleading look towards me.

As if I could help him…

Marshall's eyes widen suddenly as if he's had a revelation.

"You want my life as payment?" he squeaks out.

Lucifer lifts an eyebrow and inclines his head. "Yes. That's how these things usually go, isn't it?"

Marshall licks his lips nervously, looks to me then back to Lucifer. "Would you accept another life as payment?"

He's not about to say what I think he is, is he? No, he wouldn't. No decent human being…

Lucifer's upper lip curls with disdain but his voice sounds interested. "What are you proposing?"

Marshall is too cowardly to stop hugging his pillow so he nods his head to me instead. "Take her. Take my wife in my place."

I'm so shocked, so floored, I suck in a sharp breath that never ends.

"You want me to kill your wife?" Lucifer asks and it feels like all the warmth was just sucked out of the room.

"No, of course not..." Marshall recoils at the murderous look on Lucifer's face. "Just hold her as a deposit, an insurance, while I get you the five million."

"You mean a ransom?" Lucifer clarifies.

Marshall nods his head up and down. "Yes, yes, that's it. A ransom."

My lungs full of air, I expel it all in a loud, "How could you!" and make a lunge for Marshall.

I'm not an object he owns. He can't just trade me away to some creepy, beautiful stranger to save his own neck.

Marshall squeaks and scrambles away from me. I end up chasing him until he falls out of bed, landing on his ass.

I grip the edge of the mattress, panting with anger as I watch him scuttle backward until he bumps into Lucifer's legs.

"As much as I would love to accept your offer," Lucifer says as he pushes Marshall away with the toe of his shoe. "I'm afraid your wife is not worth the five million you owe me."

*Damn.* I blink up at Lucifer, feeling utterly conflicted. On one hand, I don't want to be given away, but on the other, it stings the ego a bit to hear I'm not worth five million dollars.

I snort though as Marshall goes to his hands and knees, kneeling in front of Lucifer to beg for mercy.

"Please," Marshall begs, reaching out and grabbing Lucifer's leg.

I'd pity him and try to help the poor bastard if he didn't just try to trade me away in his place.

"There has to be something else I can give you…" Marshall sobs.

Lucifer makes a face of disgust and looks down at Marshall like he's a bug he'd like to step on.

"Anything," Marshall wails as Lucifer kicks at him. "Anything."

I sit back on my heels and watch Marshall beg while taking the kick, wondering how all of this happened.

Lucifer's head lifts and his eyes lock on me. His features are still, utterly calm, but there's something dark stirring in the depths of his icy irises.

"Anything?" Lucifer queries.

"Yes, anything!" Marshall nods his head with sudden enthusiasm.

"I'll accept your offer," Lucifer grins at me. "If you give her to me permanently, and throw in your children."

"No, no! You can't!" I scream and I'm off the bed in an instant.

Marshall yelps and scuttles back until he's hiding behind Lucifer's legs.

Lucifer between us, blocking me, my hands clench into fists and I pant, trying to control the rush of rage that has flooded my head. I swear if Marshall offers this… this… inhuman monster my children, I'll strangle him with my bare hands.

Lucifer smirks down at me as if he finds all of this amusing. I bristle under that smirk but suddenly feel self-conscious standing so close to him. He's tall, with at least a foot on me, and I feel puny now standing in front of him.

"Well? Do we have a deal, Marshall?"

Marshall continues to use Lucifer as a shield like the

coward he is. He pokes his head out only long enough to peek at me. "Yes!"

"No!" I screech and lunge forward, reaching around Lucifer to grab Marshall.

Marshall squeaks and stumbles backward, just out of my reach.

Lucifer grabs me by the arms, stopping my forward lunge and hauls me back. Chuckling, he pins my arms to my sides and I screech and struggle, trying to escape his grasp.

"We're done here, Marshall. I suggest you leave now before I change my mind…"

"Leave? Why do I have to leave? This is my house!" Marshall protests.

Head tipping back, I glare up at Lucifer and continue to struggle. Damn, he's stronger than he looks, though it is hard to tell just how built he is under that suit he's wearing.

Once again Lucifer looks me directly in the eyes, staring into me as if he can *see* inside me. "Not tonight."

"But… but…" Marshall starts to sputter.

Lucifer's face hardens, his features as cold and harsh as the blizzard swirling in his irises. "Simon, remove him."

"No. No! I'll go!" Marshall says, panicked, and though I can't see what's going on due to the huge body blocking my view, I can hear a great deal of shuffling going on behind Lucifer.

Marshall grunts loudly and then there's a thump. "Hey! I'm going, I'm going!"

The bedroom door opens and then slams shut.

I jerk in Lucifer's arms in surprise but then feel all the fight go out of me. No matter how much I squirm, no matter how much I try to free myself from his grasp, I can't escape him. If anything, I feel like all my struggles have only tightened the grip he has on me.

Head dropping forward, I quiet my panting so I can listen

to Marshall stomping and continue to throw a tantrum about being removed from his own home.

After a minute, Lucifer sighs and I feel his grip loosen a little. "James, assist Simon. If Marshall wakes the children, feel free to make him regret it."

"Yes, boss," the second shadow answers and I don't even hear him as he walks out. I only know he's gone by the sound of the closing door.

A moment later there's some muffled arguing coming from the hallway then all goes quiet.

The seconds tick by. My panting slows as I catch my breath.

All at once I am suddenly aware that I'm alone with this strange man.

The air thickens.

Slowly, I lift my head and peer up at him. He's looking down at me so intensely I gasp.

My gasp seems to amuse him, and a slow smile spreads across his lips.

I stare at him in disbelief, my mind racing a mile a minute, trying to process everything that just happened. My mouth feels dry and my stomach is twisted. I want to believe this is a nightmare, that I'm still sleeping in my bed.

My husband didn't just trade me and our children away to save his own neck. He couldn't… He wouldn't…

Yet the fingers tightening around my arms remind me that he did.

I can't let this happen. I can't accept this. I have to protect my children. He cannot have them! I won't let him hurt them.

Gathering up every ounce of courage I have inside me, I lift my chin and say, "You can't have us. We're not objects you can own or trade away at whim. I am a *person*, a person with rights, and I will not stand for this!"

Lucifer's eyes twinkle at me and it's so condescending I just want to spit in his face.

My anger only seems to amuse him even more. Head tipping back, he chuckles with mirth and just as I start to struggle again, he lifts me up.

It only takes him two long strides and then he throws me.

I go flying through the air and land on my bed with a grunt.

He's not far behind me, and quickly I get to my hands and knees, scooting back as he approaches.

Long, strong fingers going to the bottom of his suit jacket, he begins to unbutton it as he asks me, "Who's going to stop me?"

## 3

## LUCIFER

*I* don't rush as I unbutton my suit jacket, there's no need to hurry. I have started my claiming of this woman. There is no choice now but to go on with my desires for her. Rushing now would only cause unnecessary problems for us both.

Standing before her as she kneels on the bed, I can't help but smile as she looks up at me so defiantly.

"I will!" she hisses at me.

I know she doesn't mean to look so sexual right now, I know she is trying desperately to cling to the hope that she is in control of her life. She isn't.

Pulling my coat off, I turn my back to her as I make my way over to the walk-in closet.

Raising my hand to the last of my men at the door, I say, "You may go, Peter. Secure the house before you leave."

"Yes, sir," he says as he closes the door on us.

Opening the door to the closet, I turn on the light. Spotting suitable hangers, I grin to myself as I hear the rustling of the sheets on the bed.

Stepping back out of the closet, I watch as Lily races towards the bedroom door.

"I wouldn't leave the room, Lilith," I say quietly.

Her footsteps instantly halt as she pulls open the door. One of my men is still standing guard on the other side. He takes a step toward her and she quickly closes the door, taking a step back.

"Turn around."

"Why?"

I hang my jacket on the hanger then turn to the closet again. "Don't mistake my words as a request, Lilith."

Placing the hanger on what is clearly her side, I walk back out into the bedroom.

She is standing in the spot I left her in but facing me now.

Her breath coming in deep sucks of air, she asks, "What are you going to do to my children? Are you some sort of pervert? A child mole…"

Raising my hand, I stop her train of thought right there. "No, neither my men nor I are in any way such disgusting, vile things. That is a death sentence in my circle. I will personally kill any man who harms children like that."

"Do you promise?" she asks and I can see the desperation in her eyes that I reassure her of that one fact.

"Yes, they are my children as of now. I would never allow something to happen to them."

"You can't just say something like that, people don't just become yours at your word."

"They do in my world, Lilith. This is the reality you will need to face and accept. The quicker you come to terms with belonging to me, the quicker you will find happiness in your surrender."

She doesn't say anything; her mouth is opened, shocked.

"Sit on the bed, Lilith."

She trembles slightly but moves towards the bed. Getting on it, she does her best to hide all of those pale attributes I have been devouring with my eyes.

Her pale heavy breasts pushed high in her red frilly bra. Her panties hiding her pussy between her thighs. Her ass is briefly visible as she climbs into the bed and her little thong peeks out from the back.

Grinning, I say, "I like that look on you."

Having had many women before, I've seen almost every way they can dress up their bodies and it has given me an appreciation for how a woman cares for herself.

The one before me, the one I have claimed as mine, truly does keep herself in shape. I don't see anything on her body that would ever suggest she has had children, except for the very faint lines on her hips. They look as if a cat reached up with both sets of claws and scratched her.

"Are you going to rape me now?" she asks with those sensual lips pressing together in a thin line.

"Hardly, I've had a very long night as it is." I unfasten my belt and then say, "Now that I do think about it, though, you need to change the sheets and pillowcases."

At first, she doesn't move but then she asks, "Lucifer, that's what they call you, isn't it? What kind of name is that?"

"It's what those who fear and respect me call me. For now, you will use the same name."

I think the word for how she is staring at me would be incredulous.

"There is no way I will ever—"

Again, I raise my hand in a calming motion. "Let's not be making vows or promises beyond the one already made tonight."

Rolling her eyes, she climbs back out of bed, her pale

luscious thighs moving quickly past me as she darts into the closet.

She could try to drag out the job or even try to escape right now, but to her credit, she doesn't. Moving back out of the closet, she walks to the bed where she places the linens on a chair beside it.

The rattle of my phone buzzing in my pocket pulls me from watching the little pale angel flitter around the bed. I actually dread looking down at the phone I am pulling from my pocket.

Taking my eyes off of her ethereal form almost seems like a sin.

Growling quietly to myself, I swipe my phone open to accept the call from Simon. "Yes, Simon, what is it?"

"I was calling to see if you were sure about this…"

"Absolutely, Simon, is there anything else?"

"Yeah, how do you plan on getting home in the morning?"

I chuckle at that. "Thanks for thinking of me. Have Andrew on standby for me."

Swiping the phone call off, I walk to the nightstand beside the bed, pulling my keys from my pocket. I set them and the phone quietly down.

"What exactly are you planning, Lucifer? This is crazy."

Her voice is rising as I turn to her, she is clearly not nearly as accepting of this situation as I am.

That will change.

She's mine now, there is no doubt in my mind of that. The pictures simply did not do her justice.

My eyes travel slowly up and then back down her body.

Looking back up into her eyes, I show no shame for my actions. "No, this is not crazy. This is simply what it is now."

"What am I supposed to be, your slave now? What of my children?" she asks, throwing up her hands she twists about her, gesturing to the walls surrounding us. "What about the house? Where are we supposed to live? Here with him?"

The way she says the word *him* shows the revulsion she must truly be feeling for her late husband. Well, I shouldn't be thinking of him as *late* just yet...

"No, you and our children will be coming home with me in the morning. There is no sense in disrupting their sleep tonight. Tomorrow will be soon enough to start their new lives."

Her eyes widen at me as she says quietly, "You are serious, aren't you?"

"Yes, Lilith, I am."

Slipping my fingers up into my tie, I quickly unknot the dark silver silk. Pulling it out, I set it on the dresser near the bed. Motioning for Lilith to come to me, I say, "Come. Help me get ready for bed."

She slowly comes around the bed. Her legs must feel like lead to her. Dreading what she must think will happen.

She could not be more wrong. I don't take women against their will, no, quite the opposite. I will have her begging me before I take her the way she desires deep down inside.

Stepping to my side, she looks up at me. Her eyes are so green, so wounded and scared. I know she must have an inner strength to be able to make it this far.

This is good, my woman will need to have a will of pure steel. She will only yield to me, only break to *my* desire.

Taking her hands in mine, I lift them up to the buttons of the collar on my stiff white dress shirt. "Start here."

She works the buttons down slowly, each one her fingers trying to undo but always faltering.

I know if she would only look at her work she would find the task much easier, but she can't. Our eyes are locked together. Her green emeralds so full of question, fear and resolve.

Shaking her head as the last button comes undone, she tugs the shirt out of my waistband. Pulling it off my shoulders, she runs her hands down from my clavicles to my pecs then slowly, and perhaps just a tad bit longer than she meant to, across my abs.

She drops to her knees as she assists me in removing first one dress shoe then the second, taking the socks with them. She pushes the shoes to the side of the bed.

Standing back up, her face is emotionless as her fingers dig at my belt buckle. Unfastening it, she starts to pull the band out to unfasten the button when I put my hands on hers.

"Get in bed, Lilith."

"What? Why?"

"I have no desire to do anything beyond sleep tonight."

Pushing her back against the bed, I watch as she gratefully slides herself backward, to her side of it.

I finish what she started and undo my pants, sliding them down my legs. Stepping out, I fold them neatly and put them with my shirt on the chair near the bed.

Standing there, I allow her to see her effect on me. Her eyes go wide. I turn away with a grin on my face.

Turning off the lights in the room, I come back to the bed. Slowly sliding myself between the sheets and blanket, I settle myself as close to her as I am able.

Turning on my side, I pull her close to me, her deliciously muscled ass against my cock.

"Good night, Lilith."

LILY

THIS IS MADNESS. I'm still struggling to wrap my mind around what just happened.

I first fell asleep with my husband, Marshall, in our bed, and now I'm in the very same bed with a stranger.

Lucifer's arm tightens around my waist and he pulls me into him. He's so warm, his body so inviting, it's a struggle not to relax against him.

Behind me, he's calm and silent.

In the dark I can't see him, but I can certainly *feel* every inch of him.

I'm painfully aware of the strong muscles curved around my body in a way that almost feels protective.

He's shirtless, and where his skin touches my skin it feels too good. My body likes touching him.

I shouldn't like this. I shouldn't let him trick me into dropping my defenses.

To this man holding me, I am his possession. An object he owns. Something he believes he can control, someone he believes he can bend.

But I'm only going along with this for the moment. Until I can figure out a way to get my children and myself safely out of this situation.

I'll endure anything, I'll pretend to be anything to protect them. Even if it means giving the illusion of submission.

Getting away will probably be an easier feat in the light of day. There will be more opportunities for help. More chances to make a break for it. If the children don't attend school, it will be noticed. My friends and family will become suspicious if they don't hear from me. We *will* be missed. There's a way out of this, I just have to be patient.

His scent envelopes me, spicy, warm and addictive.

I can't stop breathing him in, and I can't stop the temperature of my blood from rising.

There's something wrong with me. I shouldn't be getting turned on like this. Perhaps I'm already experiencing Stockholm Syndrome…

I squeeze my thighs together and try not to think about how heavy my breasts feel as they rise and fall with every deep breath. Or how he was unashamed of the erection tenting his pants before he climbed into bed.

Thank god he's not forcing himself upon me, and thank god he's promised not to hurt my children. Maybe I shouldn't believe his promise but I get the impression when he says something he means it.

I was tempted to put up more of a fight earlier but the look on his face made me think better of it. No, I'm better off biding my time for the moment.

Besides the man holding me, there are at least three other men present in the house that I know of. I'm not foolish enough to think I'll be able to wake Adam and Evelyn and get past all of them.

I could call the police but I know it will do no good. The more and more I come to terms with this, my new reality, my awful situation, the more and more I'm putting together the pieces.

I've heard the name Lucifer before. He and his men are notorious for their criminal exploits and their viciousness.

Every couple of weeks or so the news tends to run a story on them. There's usually some horrible crime—a murder, a massacre, or someone important gone missing—and usually Lucifer or his men are suspected of being behind it, but the authorities can never prove it.

How Marshall got mixed up with him, I'll never understand it. But I'll also never forgive him for forcing me and our children to pay for his transgressions.

Lucifer's warm breath hits the back of my neck and I shiver, my nipples tightening. His chest begins to rise and fall against me in a steady rhythm.

He's asleep… or perhaps it's a test. Either way, I'm not going to try to make a run for it… yet.

*Tomorrow, in the light of day*, I remind myself. *I'll get us away.* We'll head across the country and stay with my parents. Then, if it comes to it, we'll move to another country. Whatever it takes to get away from these awful men.

I was planning on doing that anyway after divorcing Marshall.

It's a good plan.

I just have to keep reminding myself of that. I need to bide my time.

I can get us out of this.

# 4

LILY

Somehow, someway I fall asleep. Lulled into a false sense of security by Lucifer's deep and steady breathing.

My dreams are vivid and heated. A man, I can't see his face in my dreams, is kissing my neck and caressing my breasts.

I groan and try to roll away but there's an arm locked around my waist like a vise. I can't escape, I'm trapped.

Between my thighs, my sex is throbbing madly, and I can't stop rubbing my knees together trying to ease it.

Behind me I feel something hard grinding into my ass and I thrust my hips back, grinding myself against it. I don't know what's going on.

Am I awake? Am I still dreaming?

If I'm dreaming I don't want to wake up.

I want that hardness inside me. Filling me. Stretching me.

It's been so long, so very long since I've been touched, kissed, caressed or fucked. Months and months.

I've been starved for touch and affection.

The lips kissing my neck reach my shoulder and my skin prickles with gooseflesh as the strap of my nightie is pushed down and cool air hits my breast.

A warm hand covers my breast, cupping it, kneading it. Then strong fingers pinch and roll my nipple. I bite my lip and groan, rocking my hips back.

*I never want this dream to end.*

The arm locked around my waist loosens and then a hand is sliding down, yanking up my chemise.

Dragging up my thigh and pulling my panties to the side.

I become very aware of my wetness, of the air against my throbbing flesh.

The hand on my breast squeezes hard just as the hand dragging up my thighs reaches my sex.

*Touch me. Touch me, please,* I want to beg but in this dream, I can't get the words past my lips.

A puff of hot air hits my neck and then thick fingers brush across my swollen folds. I shudder and a whimper slips past my lips.

My hips jerk forward and the hard bulge follows me, grinding rougher into my ass. The fingers drag up, spreading me open.

*Yes.*

It's been so long, my sex is aching with need and clenching down on emptiness.

I'm not sure I even remember what's it's like to have an orgasm.

A mouth touches my neck and a hard suckle is pulled back.

Then the fingers on my sex brush across my clit. Behind my eyes colors spark and flash.

My body is lit up with electric sensation.

I groan and writhe, needing more. Needing a firmer touch. I reach down, grabbing the hand, wanting to guide it.

Suddenly, teeth sink into my neck, giving me a painful nip. With a yelp, I pull my hand back.

I pant, afraid that the fingers will stop now but my fear is misguided.

A moment later, fingers touch my clit, rubbing in slow, circular motions.

I *melt*, inside I'm melting into warm gooey wetness.

Moaning, I thrust my ass back, my hips rocking in a slow, needy rhythm.

The spot on my neck that was just bit is tenderly soothed with a slow, dragging lick. The pressure of the fingers on my clit increases.

Knees locking together, my muscles lock up, tensing in anticipation.

The fingers continue to work against me, becoming fast and frantic.

The mouth on my neck is sucking and licking me as if it's trying to devour me. I swear I feel the hardness against my ass twitch.

I'm so close, I'm going to come.

I let out a low, needy groan and still just as all the pleasurable pressure reaches its apex.

All at once the fingers on my clit stop, leaving me hanging on the edge.

*No, no, no…*

I reach down again, grabbing the hand.

"Don't stop. Please, don't stop," I beg, my voice startling me as it breaks the silence.

The silence doesn't answer back, and the hand I'm gripping resists my guidance. Roughly, I'm shoved forward and my face hits the mattress.

From behind, I can feel my chemise being lifted up more and then the soft sound of fabric rubbing against skin. I try to push myself up but a firm hand pushes me back down.

Something hard touches my folds and then glides through them.

Oh fuck, I know what that is. Only the head of a cock can do that.

My hips rock back on their own volition. A weight touches my back and then presses me back down into the mattress. Lips touch my ear while the cock continues to push, slide and spread my folds.

He's slicking himself up with my wetness.

My hands grip the bed and I bite back the moan that is trying to push past my lips.

I shouldn't want this, I shouldn't.

But he left me hanging on the edge. I'm throbbing, my sex is swollen and my clit is pulsing.

I fucking *need* it.

"How long has it been, Lily?" His voice slides into my ear like a soft caress.

I press my lips together and refuse to answer the question.

The head of his cock slides up and then brushes against my clit. It's only a light touch but it's enough to cause the need inside me to increase in intensity.

"Lily..." he says, chiding me. "*Tell me*. How long has it been since a cock has been inside your pussy?"

God, the way he says the word *pussy* sounds so naughty yet so damn sexy at the same time.

He slides the head of his cock back down and prods it at my entrance.

"Did Marshall fuck you tonight?"

I tense up, hoping he pushes it further in.

With a sigh, I feel him pull back and I want to scream in frustration.

"Lily," he purrs huskily into my ear. "Did your husband fuck your pussy tonight?"

I shake my head and he rewards me by brushing his cock against my clit.

"Good girl."

He presses the head of his cock against my clit and I shudder. The pressure is so delicious.

"How long has it been? A day? A week?"

I don't want to answer him now because it fills me with humiliation.

"Lily," he growls and I feel him pull away again.

Dammit. Why is he doing this?

"Months," I whimper as he pulls completely away from me. "Maybe a whole year."

He's so still, so quiet, I almost burst into tears, fearing he finds me repulsive.

"What a fucking idiot," he declares and his warm weight presses me down again.

I can't stop the contented sigh that comes out of me nor can I stop my hips from tipping back, welcoming him as his cock finds the entrance of my pussy again.

"Are you on birth control?" he asks in a strained voice.

I shake my head. "I haven't really needed it…"

He thrusts forward suddenly, filling me up.

It's no gentle penetration. One moment there's prodding, a little bit of pressure, then I'm roughly being spread open.

But it doesn't hurt. No, there's something about it that feels so good, so raw. Like I needed this.

Pulling back, he leaves me panting with expectation. Then he slams forward again.

"Good," he finally declares. "You won't be fucking needing it."

Reaching down, he grabs me by the hips and holds me in place as he slams himself in and out of me again and again.

I come almost at once. Exploding around him. My needy, sex deprived pussy grabbing on to him so tightly I'm not sure it will ever let go of his cock again.

I cry out in pleasure, twitching and spasming, sucking him in deeper.

He growls and pounds into me harder. Fucking me like a man gone mad.

Another orgasm rocks through me, then another.

I can't stop coming.

I just keep exploding; I keep getting swept away in wet waves of bliss.

I'm not even aware of him reaching his own climax at first. I'm just suddenly full of warmth and he's roaring out that I'm *his*.

I'm fucking his.

His thrusting slows and his head falls forward, forehead leaning against my neck. His breathing is loud, uneven. My lungs struggle to take in air and my throat is raw.

It takes a few minutes for me to catch my breath.

With a groan, he pulls himself out of me and then presses a small kiss against my neck.

His weight and heat disappear, leaving me cold and shivering. I start to roll over but he stops me by grabbing me and pulling me once more into his chest. His body curls around mine and the blanket is pulled up, tucked around my shoulders.

Arms locking around me, I feel trapped.

All at once it's like a bucket of ice water has been dumped on me as the euphoria wears off.

Fuck, I didn't just do that.

# 5

## LUCIFER

Christ on a fucking pogo stick, that was the most amazing sex. Her pussy was so fucking perfect for my cock that I'm positive we were made for each other. This is fate. I was meant to have this fucking woman.

She's mine, there's no doubt in my mind about that.

The way her body crushes back against mine as we fall back into slumber feels as if I am completing something. I don't know what, but *something*.

∼

I WAKE AGAIN to the sound of my phone buzzing on top of the nightstand. Glancing at the screen, I check the time and sigh quietly.

Swiping it open to accept the call, I say quietly, "Wait."

Slipping my arm out from underneath Lilith I get out of bed as smoothly as I can. No sense in waking her up at six in the morning. I don't know what time she will get up to get the kids to school today, but it's probably not as early as six.

Putting the phone up to my ear I walk out of the bedroom and down the hall, I ask, "What is it?"

"Matthew, we have a small problem from last night with Mickey," Simon says to me.

"What's the problem? Is this seriously something you couldn't handle? You know I'm busy right now."

"Detective Sommers intercepted him as he stumbled into the precinct last night with his hand bleeding all over the floor. The fucking piece of shit wants to try and rat us out."

"For fucking what?" I growl out.

The lights are dark in the hallway and I try to keep my voice from rising. It wouldn't be a good idea to wake the kids. They don't know what their new world is yet. "It's not as if he knows much more than who we are, and how much money he owes us."

"He was willing to point you out in a lineup with myself and Andrew. He wanted to pin you for snipping his finger off."

"That fat fucking shit," I curse.

I stop outside of a partially closed door and peek in. A little blonde-haired girl is sleeping in there. With the way her body is sprawled out, she reminds me of a little broken doll.

Stepping past her door I stop at the next one. Yep, this one is a boy. He is sleeping just like his sister, but he has a small green dragon under his arm. His face, though, looks so severe and serious even when he is sleeping. Good.

"What did Sommers do with him?" I ask as I walk towards the stairs.

Time to take a tour of the house, see what kind of people live here.

"The smart thing, he yanked him out of the building and to his personal car. Quieted him down enough to try and explain the reality to him. Sommers says it isn't working though."

"He's seventy-five thousand in the hole. I don't imagine he'll be able to pay off the debt now that he is behaving the way he is."

"I agree, at this point he has become deadweight."

"What about his wife and family?" I ask.

All around me the house is very neat and tidy. The toys put up, the chairs and couches thick and comfortable. Lilith's touch can be seen throughout the house. Little feminine touches here and there.

"There are no children, his wife is a fat middle aged homemaker. She most likely has no idea her husband is in so much debt."

Lilith has pictures of her and the children all throughout the house. Sometimes Marshall is in them but more often than not he isn't. I get the feeling he doesn't spend much time here with his family.

That's a shame, really, now he never will.

Like I told Lilith—she's mine, and by proxy, the children are now mine as well.

"Have Sommers bring him to the warehouse on fifteenth street. I'll meet them there. Call Harrold to have a clean-up crew on standby."

"Understood… Matthew, about last night. Do you want to let me in on…"

"No. I'll see you at the warehouse."

"Alright," he says before I disconnect from the call.

I tour the kitchen and see that it is well used. The fridge and cabinets hold a mixture of healthy and not so healthy food in them. Looking around myself, I get the picture of a normal upper-middle-class family home.

How the hell this jackass Marshall could talk Sean into such a huge financial venture is way beyond my understanding. I knew when I was helping them that the risk was going to be too fucking high for my gain/loss ratios.

I allowed myself to get fucked out of five million dollars.

*Five million dollars.*

Marshall may think we are done with him, but we aren't. Not by a fucking long shot.

Walking back up the stairs, I move into the bedroom and stare down at the blonde-haired beauty.

Even in the pale light coming through the parted curtains I can see her finely detailed features. Her face looks like it's been sculpted from porcelain. Her high cheekbones would almost look too much if they didn't blend in so well with her cheeks. The striking pink hue of her lips are almost red.

Her lips look as if they were meant for two things, sucking my thick cock between them and kissing as hard as I can, even if it bruises them.

Sometime during the night, her hair has become even more tousled, making her look like she has been fucked senseless. I suppose she was.

I can't help but look down at her slender neck and shoulders.

The blanket covering her is an annoyance but it needs to be there I suppose. The house is warm, but in here it's a bit chilly. I bet if I were to remove the blanket, and then her bra, her nipples would be tightened into two hard diamonds.

Shaking my head, I look down at my cock. It's almost as hard as it was when I forced it completely into her this morning.

Hard, but not yet throbbing.

Dropping my boxers down my legs, I lean down kissing Lilith on the cheek. She did so well this morning.

I walk over to the master bathroom and switch on the light. It's not a large bathroom by any means, and I don't like how small this house feels.

Things are going to be much easier when we get back home.

~

THE SHOWER WAS NOT UP to my standards. I want my shower hot as fuck and with space to move around. Not some shitty tub I have to stand in.

Drying myself off, I walk out of the bathroom. It was a long night, and from the phone call with Simon, it looks like it will be even longer before I can get into some clean clothing.

I walk to where I stood before at the bed, looking down at Lilith. She looks so beautiful there. She must sense something different though because her eyes slowly open.

Staring up at me, a half smile forms on her lips before she must realize I'm the one standing before her.

Sitting up, she pulls the blankets around herself as her eyes start darting around the room.

"Good morning," I say with a smile.

"Good… What happened… You're naked," she stutters, her eyes landing directly on my cock.

Nodding my head, I finish drying my head then toss the towel back behind me towards the bathroom. "That happens when I take a shower."

"Why… we…"

"Yes, we did that this morning. I was planning on making you wait longer before serving me so well, but I could tell you have been suffering for far too long."

Her eyes grow wider as she says, "You're talking like I am your slave."

"You are, for the time being. I am sure you will eventually be more," I say as I stare down at the blanket covering her body.

Reaching down, I pull it hard from her hands.

She gasps as she asks, "What are you doing?"

"Don't ever cover yourself like that again when I want to look at you."

She sits there, her mouth opening and closing in shock.

I walk over to the chair where my clothes have been set and begin to put them on, sans the dirty boxers. It won't be the first time I have gone home without having a pair of underwear on.

"What time do you take the children to school?" I ask as I start tucking my shirt into the pants.

"Oh my god, you really were serious last night… You're trying to keep us, aren't you?"

"Yes."

"But…" She shakes her head. "I wake them at seven and drive them to preschool and kindergarten by eight."

"Good, have them there on time. I will look to see if there are more suitable schools for them later today."

Turning away from her, I sit down on the bed, reaching down to pull my dress socks onto my feet. The bed shifts as I feel her moving around.

She sits there quietly as I finish putting my shoes and socks on. "Start packing all of your belongings. I will have a moving company over here later this morning to help you pack it all up. I want you in our home today."

Standing up, I look at her, she has that dumbfounded look again. "Your life is starting over, Lilith. It's for the best if you accept it to ensure you and I are happy."

"I can't… this can't be real… I swear I'm…" she mutters as she rubs her eyes.

Her breasts rise and fall with the movements of her arms.

"One other thing, don't try going to the police," I warn. "I own them. Don't go to your friends or neighbors for help, I will kill them. If you try to escape me, you will regret it."

Grabbing my phone, I place it in my pocket.

Walking around the bed, I grab her phone from her nightstand then lean over and kiss the top of her head. She has a furious look on her face as I chuckle.

"Be good. I will see you this evening."

Walking out of the bedroom, I head down the stairs and out the front door. My driver is there waiting for me as I smile to myself.

Today should be interesting.

## 6

LILY

*Your life is starting over, Lilith,* is what Lucifer said before he left me.

But it doesn't feel like my life is starting over. It feels like my life has been ripped away from me.

Today I was going to meet with a lawyer, I was going to work towards securing my freedom from Marshall. I had a damn plan.

Now I belong to a madman.

And he is mad, there's no doubt about that. No sane person believes they can own another person, or believes they can get away with it.

How am I going to get us out of this? All kinds of possibilities run through my head as I rush through a much-needed shower.

Do I attempt to make it to the authorities? Will they be able to help me? He said he owns them. If I did contact law enforcement, I'd probably have to make contact with someone on a federal level. No doubt Lucifer has all the local law enforcement on his payroll.

And no doubt reaching out to the authorities would just draw his ire. What do I have to trade in exchange for protection?

Nothing. Nada. I don't even have any useful information.

All I know is what I witnessed last night. All I know is that my husband owes him five million dollars.

Really, Lucifer hasn't even done anything to me yet but make threats... It's my word against his, and I know how those cases tend to go. It wouldn't go in my favor.

He didn't even have to coerce me into sleeping with him. I was so starved for touch, for affection, I pretty much threw myself at him, and that's not going to help my case at all.

It just makes me look willing. God, I'm pathetic.

Scrubbing down my arms, I feel dirty and confused. And so fucking stupid.

How did I let that happen? Why did I let my body overrule my brain? I could have told him no. I could have demanded he stop. But I didn't. I just wanted *more*.

Even now, in this shower, just the memory of what we did has my blood warming. The smell of him, the feel of him, draws me in. There's something about him, something addictive, I can't even explain it. I lost all sense of right or wrong. I just wanted him so bad.

I didn't even ask him to use protection.

Shit. My hand rubs over my tummy. I haven't been on birth control for months, there's been no need for it. Marshall and I have had a dead bedroom for almost a year now.

It's not likely, but I could be pregnant with Lucifer's child now.

*Oh god, oh god.* Don't go down that road. That road only leads to madness.

I shut off the water and dry myself off.

I'm not pregnant, no way. I take a deep, calming breath and then let it slowly out.

Be reasonable, Lily.

It always took Marshall and me a few weeks before his little swimmers took. I'll just have to be sure I get away so this doesn't happen again. We just need to *go*.

What if we just make a run for it? Disappear in the wind? That feels like the best option. Maybe if Lucifer can't find us after a time he'll just give up. It's not like I'm worth much effort. He could go steal someone else's wife, or hell, find his very own.

We're not worth his trouble.

I'd just need to withdraw some money from the bank account to buy everything we need. We'll need clothes, food, and shelter. Hopefully Marshall hasn't drained all the money already. The last time I checked our savings we had about fifty grand in there.

Twisting my hair up into a messy knot, I frown at myself in the mirror. My eyes are dark and my skin is pale. I look like I haven't slept in a year.

What should I wear? When I drive the kids to school I usually just throw on some sweatpants, a baggy t-shirt and go sans makeup. I don't normally care who sees me like this, dropping off the kids isn't a catwalk moment.

If I don't want to tip anyone off to my plans I should probably keep things as normal as possible.

If I'm really lucky I can get the kids and myself out of this mess without them ever realizing what is going on or what kind of danger we're in. If I act fast enough I can spare them the confusion of our situation.

That small spark of hope gets my butt moving.

Usually getting the kids up for school is a bit hectic.

There's always something that keeps it from going smoothly so I know I have act fast.

Throwing on my morning clothes, I wake up the kids and help them get dressed for school. Neither one of them seems to be aware of anything that happened last night. They slept through it all, and they're sleepy and grumpy as usual.

Things almost feel normal as we sit down and have a cold breakfast together. Once we're full, I gather up their jackets and backpacks and step out the door. Maybe this won't be as hard as I thought.

"Mom?" Adam asks as I'm locking the side door behind us. "Whose car is that?"

"Huh?" I say before turning my head. Twisting the key in the lock, I almost snap it off.

Motherfucker.

There's a sleek black sedan parked behind mine in the driveway blocking me in.

Dammit. I should have known better.

"Mom?" Adam asks again, his big green eyes looking up at me for an answer.

Sighing, I settle my purse on my shoulder and try to sound as unconcerned as possible. "I don't know, honey. Maybe they're lost."

"Wrong house?" he suggests.

I smile tightly and nod my head. "That's probably it."

I take a step forward and the driver's side door of the black sedan pops open. Out steps a freakin' Viking dressed in a black suit.

Little Evelyn gasps and grabs onto my leg and Adam's green eyes go even wider in his head. I don't blame them. I too feel a little intimidated by the giant man staring us down. He must be at least 6'4 and is built like an NFL linebacker. Blonde hair, blue eyes, and a thick blonde beard.

His voice is rumbly and deep as he says, "Ma'am. Lucifer has asked me to drive you today."

Glancing up and down my street, my heart races in my chest and this morning's cereal is threatening to come back up. Can I get away from this guy? Do I dare involve my neighbors by asking them for help?

I don't want to get anyone innocent killed on my behalf.

Parked a couple of houses down the street I notice another black car.

Dammit.

That car isn't usually there. How many people does he have watching me? How far can we make it if we try to make a run for it now?

Probably not far.

The Viking doesn't speak another word. He just stares me down, watching me. He's big and I bet he's slow. I might be able to outrun him... if I didn't have two little children with me.

What choice do I have?

Licking my lips, I ask, "What did you say your name is?"

His hands relax and he seems more at ease as he answers. "Peter."

Tears of frustration prick at my eyes but I can't break down in front of my children, I just can't. The both of them already seem freaked out as it is.

Reaching down, I grab Evelyn's hand and say reassuringly, "It's okay, honey. There's nothing to be afraid of. Peter is just going to give us a ride to school."

"Why? Who is he?" Adam asks. He's always been an inquisitive child, and I know I have to be very careful with what I say or he'll figure out something's wrong.

"Oh, I completely forgot I need to take my car to the shop. It needs some work done."

Prying Evelyn's little fingers off of my leg, I check my

watch. "Come on. We need to hurry up or you'll be late for first bell."

Adam gives me a skeptical look and frowns. Evelyn drags her feet, literally, as I walk us up to the black car.

Peter comes around the front and opens the back door for us. Evelyn shies away but Adam only looks up at him with curiosity like Peter is an equation he wants to figure out.

"Hurry up or we're going to be late," I press and motion for Adam to enter the car ahead of me.

He enters first, reluctantly, and I pull Evelyn in with me. Peter shuts the door.

Out of sheer curiosity, I reach over and check the door by pulling on the handle. It doesn't open. The child locks must be enabled.

This just keeps getting worse and worse.

Peter slides into the driver's seat and starts up the car. Our eyes meet in the rearview mirror and he asks, "Where to?"

The police station? My parents' house? Mexico?

"Cherry Grove Elementary. Do you know where that is?"

Peter nods his head, "Yes, Ma'am."

There's a moment of quiet and then he asks, "Then Summit Academy for your daughter?"

Damn. My heart skips a beat and dread sinks into my bones. They already know where my children go to school? What else do they know?

# 7

## LUCIFER

Despite how I feel about Marshall, and my lack of trusting my intuition in regards to loaning him money, I still feel like I have come out ahead.

Looking at the house as we back out of the drive, I smirk. *Way ahead.*

Marshall didn't deserve the life he had.

Do I?

I don't really give a fuck; I'm taking it regardless.

Up in the front seat Andrew looks at me in the rearview mirror. "Where to, sir?"

"The warehouse on fifteenth."

The SUV pulls out of the driveway, slowly accelerating down the street. Looking to my side, I check the files left on the seat beside me.

It's the start of the month, where all the deadbeat shits who have borrowed money get their increase in debt. Last night was the end of the month, collection time.

"Fuck, last night was long," I mutter as I push the folder out of my lap and onto the seat.

"Yeah, it was."

"Did Mickey give you any trouble last night when you dropped him off?"

"No sir, it was a quick job. I had nothing beyond cleaning up the mess."

"Well, the fat fuck has decided that his odds are better down at the police station instead of seeing to the missing finger. Which hand did you take the pinky from?"

"That stupid motherfucker. The right hand, sir," he says angrily.

"Yeah, he was. Bet that right hand was going to cause him problems anyways," I say, snickering.

"I really did try to impress upon Mickey the seriousness of the situation, sir. I am deeply sorry if there was any way I could have prevented this."

"This isn't on you, Andrew."

"Thank you, Lucifer."

Nodding my head, I reach forward and grab the metal cup sitting in the cup holder. It's good to know my guys know what I want when they come to work for me. The black coffee warms up my stomach as I look back over at the folder.

"Shit."

"Sir?"

"I hate paperwork." I shake my head. "Paperwork and stupid people."

Life in my world is pretty much black or white, much like the legal world. Except here it's what can you do for me or how much you will be in my way. I have carefully selected those around me to be people who I can trust.

Andrew, in front of me, is one of those I have chosen as a trusted employee. He does exactly as I ask. Doesn't question orders, and will not betray me. I have instilled in him a sense of loyalty and confidence.

I don't fuck around with turncoats; I have made that very clear to each and every person who works for me. Dealing with the last person who tried to sell me out left a lasting impression on my guys. I guess that happens when you kill the guy and every single member of his family.

It's an effective message when you wipe someone's bloodline off the planet.

Andrew didn't fuck up last night, I know that. People like Mickey will happen. Somehow they think they can just back out of a commitment without there being repercussions

Thinking of issues to be dealt with, I need to keep up with Bartholomew. He has been with my group for a few years now and the thought that he would be stupid enough to be fucking around on me and my crew is almost too much.

But then again, everyone finds a Judas at least once.

Leaning forward, I say, "Andrew, I need you and Thomas to keep an eye on Bart."

Looking in the rearview mirror, he says, "As in watch out for him being a rat?"

"It's a possibility, there have been mutterings."

"Got it."

Thomas and Andrew have been with me the longest, I trust them implicitly.

Picking the file back up, I look through the ledger.

The outstanding debt was significantly cut down over the last week. But as in life, there is always some dumb fuck willing to take on more debt than he could ever repay. I try to avoid those shits.

I need to see my investments returned in full with interest if I want to remain successful.

∽

PULLING into the parking lot of the old warehouse, a couple of cars are already there waiting for me. I see Simon's Audi and then the late model Ford Explorer that belongs to Detective Sommers. There's a bloody handprint smear that slides down half the side of the vehicle that makes me wince.

For Christ's sake, who the fuck does he think we are? Some backwoods fucking clan of fucktards?

Though, to be honest, it makes me laugh on the inside a little because that hand print is missing a pinky.

I step out of my SUV and snap a finger at Andrew. "Clean that fucking shit off."

He looks at the handprint and rolls his eyes. "Jesus, Lucifer, what the fuck is he thinking?"

Shaking my head, I don't answer.

Dipping my head down into the cold wind, I head into the building. It's getting colder now that winter is finally showing its fucking face. It's been hot for way too long around here, we need the winter. The fucking heat brings out the crazies.

The door slams loudly behind me as I walk past the broken-down front desk. This building is older than me and hasn't seen an honest worker in years, but that's the beauty of it. It's still full of all that old equipment shit, making me a legitimate business owner in a sense. Even if I don't have any employee's here.

Going past all the stamp presses and sheet metal cutters, I head to the back of the building. It's not hard to figure out where all the action is. I just follow the fucking blood trail like Hansel and Gretel.

Another shake of my head, I'm getting more pissed as I see how much blood and fucking DNA evidence there is on the shit around me.

When I get to the back of the large building, I see Mickey

bound to a chair with a gag crammed far into his mouth. There's snot and tears all over his face. He looks like shit.

The detective isn't much better. He has a black eye forming and his usually neat, orderly suit is bloody and ripped in spots.

"What the fuck happened to you, Sommers?" I ask as I come up to the trio.

Simon is the only one who looks normal.

Simon lifts his brows at me as I give a small nod of my head. Putting his hand inside the inner pocket of his coat, he pulls out a large envelope that is stuff full of cash.

"This piece of shit," Sommers growls before lashing out with a fist at Mickey's face. "Fucking fought me the whole damn way."

"I can tell," I say. "Did you not see the fucking bloody handprint on your Explorer?"

"Shit, seriously?"

Nodding my head, I watch as Simon hands the money over to Sommers. "Yeah, and all the fucking DNA you left on the way in here."

Shaking his head, he looks at Mickey. "You stupid fat fuck!"

Sommers punches a barely coherent Mickey twice before he steps back. Spitting on the man, he says "You fucking ruined my damn suit, you pile of shit."

Turning to me, Sommer's has a penitent look on his face as he says, "Lucifer, I'm sorry about the mess he left coming in here."

"Don't worry about it. Did anyone at the precinct see Mickey? Anyone going to be an issue?"

"Nah, all my guys were on duty last night." Putting the envelope in his jacket pocket, he pats it. "Won't be a problem at all."

"Good," I say and then look at Mickey. He's slowly

coming around now. "Mickey, that was fucking stupid. You should have come to me if you couldn't pay me back. Now you've caused way too many problems. I tried to give you a lesson last night, but all you've shown me is that you're too stupid to fucking learn."

Shaking my head, I walk over to Simon. Motioning with my hand, I accept the nine-millimeter pistol he places in my palm.

"Mickey, your fat twat of a wife is going to die because of what you did last night."

Eyes bulging, he screams into the gag. His words are too garbled to understand, but I bet he is saying some sad shit to me. Least I hope he is because he fucked up bad enough that he is ending her life too.

Aiming the pistol at his head, I pull the trigger twice. Each bullet slams through his skull, exploding out the back with blood, bone and brain matter.

Turning to the two men beside me, I say, "Simon, have this cleaned."

Simon looks unfazed by the situation. Sommers is a shade paler than normal for a black man but he wisely keeps his mouth shut. That's good, I don't want to kill him. I'm pretty sure he knows that too, especially since he knows I just made him a knowing accessory to murder.

Putting my hand on his shoulder, I turn him from the gory scene and start walking with him as I hear Simon making a phone call.

"How's Jeanie and Alicia doing? Alicia still planning on heading to that ivy league college?"

"Yeah, she is trying hard to make sure Jeanie and I have no retirement money left, I swear."

Laughing, I say, "Well, if she needs help getting into Yale let me know. I know a couple of their board members. I should be able to get her in and lessen some of that financial burden."

Nodding his head, he says, "I will."

∼

GETTING INTO THE VEHICLE, I look to Andrew as I rub my hands. The Explorer looked much better when I came out of the building. "Good job."

"Thanks, Lucifer. Where to next?"

"Let's wait for Simon to come out, then downtown."

We sit there for only a couple of minutes before Simon comes out of the building, zipping his winter coat up. Walking over to our vehicle he comes up to my window.

Rolling it down, I say, "Meet me downtown at Fifty-Three for breakfast, after you get the shit set to be cleaned here. I'm fucking starving. Then we need to go to a club on forty-eighth street I'm looking into buying."

"The strip club? What's it called, Lucky Tails?" he asks.

"Yeah, that's the one," I say, smiling.

"Fuck, how many strip clubs can a man own?"

8

LILY

*D*ropping the kids off for school is a surreal experience, and really drives home the point that I no longer have any control of my or my children's lives.

Since I can't open the back doors from the inside of the black sedan, I have to wait for Peter to open them for us like he's some kind of fancy chauffeur.

It'd be more fitting if he was dressed up as a prison warden.

We drop off Adam first. There are a few looks as we pull up to the curb and Peter comes around to let us out. This is a nice school but it's not *that* nice. We're upper-middle-class around here, not Wall Street.

Adam is only in kindergarten but he hates being babied so I stay in the car and just watch him until he disappears through the school's front doors.

Usually he's in a rush to get inside and meet up with his friends before the first bell, but today he pauses in front of the doors and glances back, his little face pinched in concern. It makes him look so much older.

I hate it.

I know he knows something is going on, and he's too smart not to figure this out on his own eventually. If I can't get us out of this mess today, I don't know what I'm going to tell him.

How do I protect him from this?

I wave from within the car but I'm not sure he can see me. Eventually, one of his friends comes up and slaps him on the back, drawing his attention away. I release a little sigh of relief as they walk into school together. At least in there I know he's safe.

Evelyn, on the other hand, is only four and I have to walk her up to the doors of her preschool.

I feel every eye of the mommy clique turn on us as we pull up.

Peter opens the door for Evelyn and me. I step out and some of the mommies are gasping. Yeah, I look like a hot mess so I just ignore all the stares and rush her inside. I help her hang up her coat and put her lunch box away.

After hugging her goodbye, I press a kiss to the top of her head and tell her to have a good day.

She hugs me back and tells me cheerfully, "You too, mommy." Before turning around and skipping off to play with the toys.

Peter is waiting for me when I walk back out. Standing in front of the back door, his eyes narrow at me and he crosses his arms over his chest as I eye the group of mommies standing near the entrance.

I could walk up to them, join in the conversation. Let them question me about the car and driver. Maybe drop a few hints...

No, no, it wouldn't be right to drag anyone else into this

mess. Besides, who's going to believe me? I'm not sure I'd believe myself.

With a sigh of resignation, I lift my chin into the air and walk back to the car, climbing in. Peter shuts the door behind me and without my children with me the sound is so much more ominous.

Silently, he drives me back to my house and there's already a moving truck parked in the driveway.

Shit.

Again, I have to wait for Peter to open my door, and he follows close on my heels as I walk up to my house. All the doors are open, letting all the heat out, and there's another beefy guy in a suit hanging out in my kitchen.

"James," Peter rumbles and nods his head at the man.

"Peter," the man grins back before popping a strawberry in his mouth.

James is leaning against the island counter and has a spread of bagels, fruit, and muffins in front of him.

Peter breaks away from me and walks up to the island, perusing the breakfast spread.

Swallowing down his strawberry, James turns his dark eyes on me and asks, "Hungry?"

Crossing my arms over my chest, I quickly shake my head.

"Are you sure?" Peter asks, surprising me. He picks up a bagel and waves it at me. "You don't want a bagel? Or a muffin?"

I shake my head again and both men frown at me like I just insulted them.

I don't have to justify myself to them, yet I explain, "I already ate breakfast with the kids."

"Ah," Peter says and then he smiles. He takes a huge bite out of the bagel in his hand.

"Would you like some juice?" James asks, pointing to the pitcher on the counter.

I shake my head.

"Coffee?"

"Yes, please," I nod, totally feeling the irony of them offering me food and drink in my own kitchen.

"How do you like it?" James asks as he walks around the island and begins opening my cabinets.

Watching him root around in my stuff annoys the hell out of me, especially because he acts as if he has every right to do it. This is my house and these are my things, dammit.

But what can I do about it?

Stomp my foot and throw a tantrum?

"The mugs are in the cabinet above the dishwasher," I tell him after he fails to find them on his own.

He flashes me a grin, "Thanks."

He pulls down two mugs. One mug reads, *World's Greatest Mommy*, while the other says *Coffee Makes Me Poop*.

"How do you like your coffee?" he repeats, walking up to the coffee maker and filling both cups from the carafe.

"Black."

He pushes the *World's Greatest Mommy* mug towards me, across the counter. I'll have to get closer to them if I want it. Lifting the other mug up to his lips, he watches me with interest before taking a sip.

"Hey, where's my cup?" Peter asks.

"Pour your own, I'm not your bitch," James smirks at him.

Grumbling, Peter walks over to the cabinet, pulls a mug down and fills it from the carafe.

I shuffle forward, pick up my mug and shuffle back, cradling it in my hands.

James grins at me, looking amused as I finally take a sip of it. "The movers are on standby all day. Just tell them what you want boxed up and they'll take care of it."

I take another sip of my coffee, savoring the warm, bitter taste. I'll need all the energy I can get to get through this.

"What exactly should I be packing up?" I ask.

Seriously, what's the point of all of this?

"Anything you want to keep."

James' dark eyes harden towards me as I say, "This is my house and I want to keep it."

He shakes his head and lowers his cup to the counter. "Lucifer wants you to pack your things. His orders are final. You will not be coming back."

So far, I think I've been holding it together pretty well. I mean, a stranger has entered my house, forced my husband out, and thinks he now owns me and my children. Given everything that's going on, I'd say I've been pretty damn level-headed about all of this.

But having James, another stranger, tell me I will not be coming back to my own house just makes me snap. Maybe it's the way he says it, like he doesn't expect me to protest or put up a fight about it, like he's taking my cooperation for granted.

Or maybe it's just the fact that he's walking around my house like he owns it that pushes my last button.

I launch my cup of hot coffee at his head and he ducks just in time. The cup goes soaring over his head and smashes against a cabinet.

"Fucking hell," he curses and straightens back up, staring me down.

I'm frozen, rooted to my spot. Did I just do that?

Our eyes meet and I'm so upset, so freaked out about everything, about what I just did, my chest is tight and I feel like I can't catch my breath.

Are they going to hurt me now?

Why the fuck did I just do that? Why am I so stupid?

My eyes prickle with tears but I don't want to cry,

dammit. I don't want to give these assholes that satisfaction. They're so not worth it.

I manage to suck in a big breath and just hold it, keeping it all in.

Peter erupts into loud, booming laughter and a moment later James joins him.

All at once I can move again.

I take off running, as fast as my feet will carry me. I fly down the hallway and hit the stairs that lead to the upper floor.

Behind me I can hear James laughing and cursing. "Fuck, that shit burns."

Peter laughs even louder. "You better ice that."

"Shit. I didn't see that coming. That was close."

"Yeah, she almost took your head off. Looks like Lucifer has got himself a little hellcat."

~

I SPEND the morning locked in my bedroom. I consider changing my clothes and putting makeup on, but fuck it. I don't care what people think, and I sure as hell won't go out of my way to make myself look good for him.

I keep expecting Lucifer to come knocking on my door at any minute, or one of the guys to try to pay me back, but thankfully the house remains quiet. They seem to be leaving me to my own devices.

I dig into Marshall's side of the closet, searching for anything that he may have kept hidden. If he borrowed five million dollars from a guy like Lucifer, he must have been into some pretty shady shit.

I spend at least a couple of hours dumping out all of his things. Boxes from high school. Drawers full of odds and ends. I search through his clothes, checking all his pockets. I even lift his side of the mattress.

In the end, I come up empty-handed. If there's anything in this room he has it well hidden.

The house is so quiet that by the time my stomach starts to rumble for lunch I have enough courage to open the door and peek out my head.

The hallway beyond my room is empty.

I tiptoe down the stairs. I can hear quiet voices coming from the kitchen.

"I can understand why he decided to keep her, she's fucking hot. What I can't understand is why he's keeping the children," Peter says.

"He can't rightly kill her children and expect her to deal with it."

"I guess so, but shit, this whole thing is messed up."

"Yeah."

"If he wanted to keep a woman, he could have kept that blonde of Hammond's. She didn't have any kids."

"I don't know what he's thinking, but he's the boss. He knows what he's doing."

"Still… it feels like an awfully big risk just for some pussy. I'd feel better if we just stuck to protocol and killed them."

"It's not up to us, so quit fuckin' talkin'."

"Do you hear something?"

I try to creep quietly back up to my room but James appears at the bottom of the stairs.

Our eyes meet and he grins. "Hey."

My heart quickens with panic and I almost trip trying to walk up the stairs backward.

"Hey, no hard feelings, okay?" He takes a step up the bottom step. "We've got lunch in the kitchen if you're hungry. Ordered out some sandwiches."

I shake my head.

These men are complete psychopaths. One moment

they're talking about how much easier it would be if they just killed me and the next they're offering me sandwiches.

He frowns and casts a look behind him as Peter appears behind his back.

"Listen, if you don't start packing up soon, everything is going to be left behind," Peter says.

"Yeah, take it or leave it. We're not coming back."

I continue to walk backward.

James' face hardens with frustration and he growls out, "I mean it. You're going to lose all your shit."

Is there anything I want? I was planning on leaving it behind anyway, it's just stuff. Why do they care anyway?

I reach the top of the landing and keep on walking.

Peter snorts and James nods his head at him. "Yeah, she's planning on making a run for it."

My stomach feels like it just dropped right out of me.

"No, I'm not," I gasp, turning back.

James smirks smugly at me. "Only a person planning on running wouldn't care about all of their things."

Peter nods at James and threatens, "I'll put in a call to Lucifer."

Dammit.

"All of it," I croak as Peter starts to walk away.

James' smirk sharpens. "What was that?"

I take a deep breath and then say more clearly. "All of it. I want all of it."

Bastards. They are so getting a kick out of this.

Peter stops and turns back. He grins triumphantly. The two assholes just played me well. "I'll get the movers in here so they can get started."

I take another step back, planning on hiding out in my bedroom again.

"You'll need to stick with us while the movers are in here," James says.

My first reaction, of course, is to shake my head.

Peter's grin is downright feral as he says, "We wouldn't want anyone to have an accident."

What the fuck does he mean by that? Is he implying I could have an accident? Or one of the movers?

James takes another step up and holds out his hand. "Come on. Come have some lunch with us. You look like you need it."

My stomach chooses that exact moment to growl loudly and I can feel my cheeks burning with embarrassment.

I want to ask him if he's going to kill me but I don't want to give away that I eavesdropped on their conversation. From what I heard, it sounds like at least Peter would prefer to kill us but he can't.

James nods at me encouragingly and Peter disappears back into the kitchen

I suppose starving myself isn't going to do me or my children any favors. I take another step down the stairs and tense up. When James doesn't jump at me and backs up instead I feel comfortable enough taking another step.

"I'll even pour you another cup of coffee, just don't throw it at my head again, okay? Wasting coffee is sacrilege," He grins as I reach the bottom, obviously trying to make me feel more comfortable with him.

I envision doing just that and feel my lips pull into my own feral grin.

"Shit," James grins right back. "You're getting your coffee in a sippy cup for that."

\* \* \*

I spend the rest of the day in the kitchen, munching on sandwiches and pretending to mind my own business. The movers flow in and out of the house, and each box that is removed feels like they're taking a little piece of my soul with it.

At one point, there's a loud crash in the family room and I can hear one of the movers cursing angrily. James, Peter, and I head into the room to investigate what happened. The family portrait I had hanging above our fireplace was dropped and the glass of the frame shattered.

"Stay back, ma'am," the mover warns me. "There's glass everywhere."

Seeing the last portrait of Marshall, me and the children I had taken fractured into pieces on the floor feels like an omen.

I cover my mouth with my hand and take a step back.

"I'm real sorry about that, ma'am. The company will make it right," the mover apologizes.

James and Peter both look at me and take in my distressed state.

James curses under his breath, "Fuck."

It's obvious that me being upset has pissed them off.

Peter takes a threatening step towards the mover and I just know he's going to hurt him or something.

"No!" I cry out and jump forward, grabbing him by the arm.

Peter glances back at me sharply and I plead with him, "Please, don't. It was just an accident."

The mover shifts uneasily. "Yeah, it was just an accident.... I'm real sorry. The company will pay for this. It will come out of my check."

"No, no, that's okay. Just throw it in the trash." I drop my hand from Peter's arm and cross my arms over my chest. "I didn't want to take that portrait with me anyway." I shrug my shoulders and try to look as nonchalant as possible. "Seriously, where would I even hang it?"

The mover lets out a relieved breath. I force a smile at him. "I was just worried that you were hurt."

The mover shakes his head. "Nah. I'm fine, ma'am."

This seems to satisfy Peter and James. We all turn and head back into the kitchen together without incident.

My heart, though, races for another couple of minutes and I feel like I'm going to be sick. It's a long time and a lot of steady breathing before I feel better again.

When it's time to finally pick up the kids, I nearly run out the door, eager to see them.

Picking up Evelyn is easy, she doesn't question the black car or the driver. She just babbles away about her day and all the different toys she played with.

Adam, on the other hand, is even more suspicious.

I can tell he wants to ask me questions when he climbs in the car but he seems hesitant to do it in front of Peter.

Like I said, sometimes he's too smart for his age.

Adam broods beside me silently and I do my best to look cool and calm for them.

"Mom, did we do something bad?" Adam asks as the car slows and I look at him with confusion.

"No, honey. We didn't do anything bad. Why would you ask that?"

He points out his window. "Then why are we pulling into a prison?"

I scoot closer to him and peer over his head.

Damn. The place we're pulling up to does indeed resemble a prison. There's a fence and a guard manning it, wearing an automatic rifle over his shoulder—out in the open. Beyond the gate there's a little guard shack and I can see the dark silhouettes of more guards.

How much protection does one man need?

The gate opens and the car rolls slowly through it as the guard waves us on. Up the long driveway, sitting on the hill is a house that's definitely big enough to qualify as a mansion. There's a fountain and everything in front of it.

As we pass the little guard shack, a couple of guards step

out and peek at the car curiously. I turn around and watch the gate slide to a shut behind us.

Shit. Fuck. Shit.

Despair sets in as I realize we're never getting out of this unless he lets us.

# 9

## LUCIFER

Strip clubs have a certain smell to them, one that is unique to only them. It's a mixture of beer, tobacco smoke, pussy, and desperation.

The one I'm in right now has that in spades.

The full tour has left me with a rotten taste in my mouth. It has the usual smell, but it also has the added coat of grimy sleazebag and jizz.

The owner is as questionable as the rules of no extras in the private dance rooms. I was propositioned the moment I sat down at one of the tables next to one of the stages.

Shit, Simon refuses to sit down at the table period. Instead, he stands behind me to one side. I have to laugh at that.

With three tumblers of whiskey in his hand, the owner plops himself down in a chair across from me.

His voice is gravelly from too many years of alcohol and

smoking. "What do you think of the club? It's got some charm, right?"

For an early afternoon shift, it's surprisingly full of dancers and customers. The location isn't too bad for where it's located within the city. Looking around myself, I see it has both blue-collar workers and suits.

I can hear Simon, though, scoff loudly over the pounding music. "If you like contracting fifteen types of diseases. I can feel them climbing on me just standing here."

He has the rights to it, though, the place is filthy. I can't imagine what it would look when they turn on all the lights.

"What do you want for it outright?"

Charles, the owner, studies me for a long moment. "One point two million."

Shaking my head at him, I lean forward and say, "Not a chance. I know about your debts with the Morelli family. Five hundred and fifty, and I clear all debts with them."

His cheeks puff out for a moment before saying, "One million, and any lower is an insult."

Shaking my head, I stand up from the chair. "Have a good night."

"Lucifer, wait. Seven hundred fifty thousand."

Nodding my head, I say "After a building inspection goes through, and I have one of my men check over your books with the actual reported earnings. I don't want a single surprise."

Nodding his head, he says, "Deal."

"You won't be staying on in any capacity."

Rolling his eyes, he says, "What, ya don't trust me?"

"Fuck no."

Walking out of the building and into the sun, I grin. I have been watching the place for the last couple months. As soon as I remove the crackhead dancers and get a few good ones in, that place is going to be an earner. Its location is just about perfect.

All I need to do is to take a good scrub brush to it.

"Simon, get the deal written up and finished. I want it taken over as soon as possible."

"You're really going to buy that STD shit hole from hell?"

"Yeah, it's going to be an earner."

"Only if you burn it to the ground and claim it for insurance."

"Want to make a bet on it?"

Sighing loudly as he climbs in the front seat, he says, "No, Lucifer."

Laughing, I look at Andrew. "Care to make a wager, Andrew?"

He just shakes his head. "No, thank you, sir. I prefer to actually keep my money."

They know me only too well. I know what it takes to make a business like that thrive and it won't be much. A change of management, new dancers who aren't all coked up, clean the place from top to bottom and a bit of word of mouth. We will be pulling in a decent income in months.

∽

ANDREW PULLS us into the compound as the moving truck for Lilith pulls out of the gate.

Good. I'd prefer not to deal with strangers inside my home any longer than I must. Especially now that I have to have the whole place swept for bugs and surveillance equipment.

I wouldn't have made it this far in life if I slacked on security. Security, in fact, is my top investment.

Andrew drives me to the front door where he drops me off.

It's been a long night and today was mildly stressful with the whole Mickey situation. Not to mention all the other odds and ends I have to see to with the daily business.

Opening the front door, I pause in confusion as Paul comes barreling down the stairs with a little girl screeching behind him. She is stomping down each stair as she holds up a small teddy bear in one hand and a pink brush in the other.

Coming to an instant halt in front of me, Paul says, "Boss... This isn't... well... she's trying to make me do another tea party."

Looking at him, I don't think I comprehend the words that come out of his mouth until I look down at his hands.

Paul looks like most of the men I surround myself with in size and build—which is large and capable of anything thrown at him.

But when I look at his bright pink fingernails, I instantly ask, "What the fuck happened to your fingers?"

"Awww, you say bad word!" The little girl giggles as she darts between Paul's legs.

Looking down at her sticky looking face, I take a step backward. My eyes look up to Paul. "What's happening here?"

"Well... Sir..." He lifts his hands up in a surrendering gesture. "Evelyn's mother let her loose on me."

Sighing, I nod my head. Looking down at the girl who is staring at me wide-eyed, I ask, "Where is your mother, dear?"

Pointing through the house, towards the kitchen, she looks up at Paul and slaps him right in the balls. A whimper comes out of him as his eyes cross.

"My god!" he shouts out as he looks up at the ceiling.

Bending down to pick up the little girl in my arms, I think —*good for her*. She needs to know how to defend herself.

"It's your penance, Paul. All those late nights with dubious women."

I carry the little girl in my arms as she wraps one arm around my neck. Sitting there, she asks, "You gonna say bad words again?"

"No, not right now. Maybe if I get really mad. I use a lot of them."

"I'm gonna tell mommy if you do," she says in a matter-of-fact voice.

"Well, I'm the boss here, dear. I don't think that's going to be an issue."

Walking into the kitchen, she giggles as I set her down, saying, "No, I'm the boss."

I see Lilith in her baggy sweatpants and way oversized t-shirt. She can't be aware of how sexy she is standing there with her hip cocked to the side as she talks quietly with her son. He looks far more upset than the little girl I just had in my arms.

Fuck, I didn't think I had a thing for MILF's but I do looking at her ass pushed out there, her sexy waist barely hidden in the baggy pants.

Turning to see what's happening, the profile of her face stirs a possessive hunger deep down in my loins. I can feel my cock wanting to stir from the memories of this morning.

Her toned ass slamming back against my hips as I buried myself deep inside of her.

Being possessive is nothing new for me, but I can feel how fast she is becoming an obsession for me.

Fuck, if the children weren't present right now I would order the house cleared just to take her right there on the counter. Push her chest down on the countertop as I rip her panties away before I thrust my fat cock deep into her tight pussy. Slap her ass as I slam in as deep as I can.

She turns fully to me and her full lips turn into a frown as she spots me. "Oh."

Taking my suit jacket off, I fold it over one of the chairs next to the island.

Looking between her and Adam, I ask, "Am I interrupting anything?"

Nodding her head, she says, "Yes. Adam was asking why we moved from our home to here."

Looking to Adam, I say, "This is your new home, Adam."

His eyes go wide as he looks to his mother. "Who is he mom?"

Sighing, Lilith turns so she can face us both. "This is Luci—"

Cutting off in the middle, she looks right at me. Hmm, I guess I haven't told her my full name. "I'm Matthew Harper, Adam,"

"Do you live here too?" he asks.

He's a serious boy, I can tell. His eyes have that worldly old man quality to them. He isn't as trusting as it appears his sister is.

Taking a moment, I stare at him. He's going to be far more curious of what is happening.

How would I have wanted to be spoken to at his age, if something like this happened to me? He is going to be harder to win over, and if I'm going to be able to get Lilith to fully accept this situation I need to ensure both children are on my side.

"This is our home now. As your mother and I have come to an agreement, it's yours as well."

"What about my old house?"

"That belongs to Marshall…" Taking a moment to think, I say, "How about this? Tomorrow, you and I will sit down in our office after I get home and go over every question you have. I want you to think of everything you can." Looking at his hands, I ask, "Can your write yet?"

"A little. It's still very shaky."

"Okay. You will write down all of your questions and we will go over them together. Just you and I. I want you used to having me around all the time."

*Unlike his father*, I think to myself.

Looking from his mother to me, he looks more confused now than scared. "Okay."

I look back to Lilith and her small frown has turned to a look of frustration. I ask, "How was your day?"

Leaning in, I kiss her on the cheek briefly while I take a deep breath of her. She smells so good, it's a heady type of smell, almost hypnotic.

Standing stiff, she says, "We need to talk."

"Yes, we do. But Rosa will be here in a few minutes to begin dinner. We can talk after the kids are in bed. I need a shower, today was very long and I'm looking forward to getting into some clean clothes."

∼

GLANCING AROUND THE BEDROOM, I take in the boxes sitting against the walls, unpacked. It looks like Lilith isn't fully accepting the situation. That's to be expected I guess. Though if this morning was any indication of how things will be, I believe she will become adjusted to her new life soon enough.

I walk back into the kitchen. Fresh from the shower, a pair of khakis and a polo have replaced my suit and tie.

My father never changed from suits and ties, never. He was far too rigid in his ways. I need to loosen up if I want the children to look at me as anything beyond their taskmaster.

Since I now have a family living here, I suppose I will have to be here more often than normal as well. Since I have taken on this house, I have used it as a place to lay my head, but that was the extent of it most of the time.

Rosa, the housekeeper and cook, has the kitchen filled with delicious smells. Steam is coming from the stove as she and Lilith talk.

Coming up behind Lilith, I wrap my arms around her waist. She stiffens against me as I nuzzle her neck. Placing a very light nip on her skin there, I say, "Go shower and get ready for dinner."

Pulling away from my arms, she looks at me wide-eyed, "What?"

"You need to go shower then dress for dinner."

"What do you mean?"

"Which part are you not understanding?" I ask. I'm confused. How is this even a question I need to address?

"What's wrong with what I'm wearing? And what's with telling me what to do?"

"You're to be dressed for dinner. Sweatpants and ratty shirts are not dinner attire."

Taking hold of her hand, I pull her through the kitchen doors to the hall. Then I pull her along the route through the house to our bedroom.

This act of rebellion will not do at all.

Walking into the bedroom, I let go of her hand and pointing to the boxes, I say, "This is will not do. Unpack your things tomorrow. Make sure the children's clothes are removed from the boxes as well. I want them cleaned. Tell Rosa before she leaves that you have a very big problem with your laundry and she will have it done."

"I want all the boxes emptied in the next three days. Anything with Marshall on it or that belonged to him will be destroyed or returned. Your choice on what to do with those items."

Next I point to the shower. "You are to be presentable for dinner. I do not ask you to dress formally but whatever you put on in the morning is not acceptable. Especially this."

I consider her emerald eyes, they are on fire right now. She looks so angry I can tell she is barely containing her anger.

"You are absolutely beautiful. I want to see that beauty when I come home, not some slobby sweatpants."

Leaving the room, I head back down the stairs to find the children. A nanny might be a good idea to have in the house. Someone who can make sure they are not destroying the place.

Dinner is a quiet affair with just us four until Evelyn decides we need to talk. She begins to ask every single question that comes to her little pink mind.

She bounces from why do we like green beans to how come her classroom has more chairs than desks. I didn't know a child could ask so many questions while cramming food in her mouth so often she looks like a chipmunk.

Adam keeps looking at me curiously but keeps to himself while he eats. His only question is, "Will I still go to the same school?"

At the same time Lilith and I both answer differently. "Maybe," and "Yes".

Looking to her, I say, "Maybe. It depends on what the reports come back with."

"No, they will stay in their schools. It's what they know and they have friends there."

Frowning, I look to Adam. "What do you want?"

"I want to stay."

"We will talk about it tomorrow."

Looking at me with the anger that hasn't left her eyes since I sent her to clean herself up, Lilith says, "We will be talking about it tonight."

Nodding my head, I say, "Among other things."

## 10

LILY

On one hand, my children seem to be completely oblivious to the truth of our situation, and that's a godsend. On the other hand, I hate deceiving them, and I definitely hate that they're already starting to settle in.

I do not want to be here for the long term. I want my freedom back, I need it. We're out of here the first chance we get.

Lucifer told Adam that he and I have an agreement, and we most certainly do not. He gave me no choice in any of this, and the fact that he's going to pretend that he did just makes me seething mad.

I want to tell him off but I have to restrain myself in front of the children.

Dinner is tedious, and the only bright spot is Evelyn's gabbing. I keep expecting her to ask about her daddy but she hasn't. I suppose it's a testament to how truly awful of a father Marshall is.

The food is bland and tasteless. It's not the cook's fault, this meal of lamb and risotto is worthy of any five-star restaurant, it's just that I have no desire to eat. I'm too stressed out to taste anything.

Throughout the meal, I focus my attention on Adam and Evelyn, trying to ignore Lucifer like he's some dark shadow at the head of the table of little importance.

But each time I turn my face to speak with Evelyn, I catch a glimpse of him out of the corner of my eye and my attention is instantly drawn to him.

The way he stares at me openly with eyes full of hunger has a way of making me feel completely naked.

I hate it, I swear, but my body betrays me. Throughout dinner I'm shifting in my seat and crossing my legs, willing the ache building up inside of me to go away.

I'm attracted to him, there's no point in denying it. How could I not be? He's ethereally beautiful yet strong and masculine.

And the fact that he desires me? It does things to me. Things that make me feel wicked and dirty. Things that make me feel like an awful mother and a wanton woman.

It doesn't seem to matter how much I psychologically can't stand him; I'm physically drawn to him. Somehow, I'm weak to him, and it terrifies me.

He made me change for dinner. He downright sneered at my sweatpants. I was half tempted to defy him and see what he would do about it.

But then I thought it would be more satisfying to best him at his own game.

At this moment, I'm seriously regretting that decision.

The children are finished with dinner so we all rise so I can go through the motions of getting them ready for bed.

I feel Lucifer's eyes all over my body as I walk over to

Evelyn to take her by the hand. He comes up behind me and all the little hairs on the back of my neck stand on end

I stiffen as his hand goes to the small of my back.

Before dinner, I slipped on the sexiest thing I own. A black little strappy dress I bought last year for my six-year anniversary. I never got to wear the dress because Marshall never came home so it just hung in my closet, sad and unused. Paired with a set of sexy black heels and a little bit of makeup, I look like a completely different woman.

Lucifer leans close, brushing my hair away from my ear. His breath is warm and I have to fight the shiver that's shooting down my neck. "I'll be in our room. We can have our *talk* once you're done putting the children to bed."

He leans back and looks into my eyes, checking for my compliance. Right now, right here, the full strength of his gaze is too intense.

I look away, focusing on Adam. He's watching us with curiosity, a little wrinkle between his brows and a frown on his lips.

"The children need to be bathed. It may be some time..."

Out of the corner of my eye, I see Lucifer nod. "I'll be waiting. Take as long as you need."

He presses a kiss against the top of my head and steps back.

I really wish he wouldn't do that! I really wish he wouldn't treat me with such familiarity, such affection, especially in front of the children.

"Good night, Evelyn. Sweet dreams," Lucifer says.

"Good night," Evelyn chirps cheerfully. "Sweet dreams!"

"Good night, Adam," Lucifer nods at Adam.

Adam stares at him for a long moment before nodding back. "Good night."

Leading Evelyn by the hand, we walk past Lucifer and

begin to ascend the stairs. Suddenly Evelyn twists in my hand and calls out, "Oh, I forgot! Don't' let the bedbugs bite!"

Lucifer laughs.

\* \* \*

Adam is of an age now where he prefers to take showers. He's cleaned, brushed, dressed and ready for bed within minutes. Evelyn, on the other hand, still needs a bath. She loves bubbles and to play, so it's almost an hour before I have her dry, brushed and tucked into her new bed.

Sometimes Evelyn needs me to stay with her while she falls asleep, and tonight I'm pretty much counting on it. After all, we're in a new house, in a new bed. She's bound to be a little frightened.

Unfortunately, she closes her little eyes as soon as I have her tucked underneath her blanket and she's asleep within seconds. I suppose all the excitement of the day wore her out.

Too bad I'm not just as tired. I feel wide awake and wired, like I've been caffeinated.

Still, I lay beside her in the bed for a long time. Reluctant to make my way to Lucifer. Reluctant to be alone with him again.

I stare at the ceiling, reliving my day. It's all so weird it hardly feels real. Did all of that really happen, or am I going crazy?

Maybe this is all some kind of nightmare and I'll wake up in bed beside Marshall.

But then, wouldn't that be a different kind of nightmare?

Finally, after I've been in bed with Evelyn for at least an hour I can lie still no more, I press one last kiss to her forehead, slide out of her bed and pick my heels off the floor.

Barefoot, I pad quietly down the carpeted hallway, hoping Lucifer is not waiting for me behind that bedroom door. If I'm lucky, I've taken so long he grew bored or tired.

Taking a deep breath, I steel myself and turn the handle. The door swings open easily and I step inside.

Lucifer is sitting on the edge of the massive canopy bed that dominates the room, bent over my phone.

His head pops up as I step inside. "Close the door."

God, I really don't want to be alone with him, and it's not because I don't trust him… it's because I don't trust myself.

Lucifer lowers my phone to his lap and repeats, "Close the door, Lilith."

I push back at the door in frustration and it slams shut a little louder than I intended. I wince at the sound and Lucifer's icy eyes narrow.

He spreads his legs a little. "Come here."

My body freezes and I just can't bring myself to take that first step forward even though there's something in his voice that tugs at me, that makes me want to obey him. "I thought we were going to talk?"

"Come here, Lilith," Lucifer demands again.

There's that tug again. A string inside me tightens.

I shake my head. I can't…

"Lilith," he growls impatiently.

My fingers relax and I drop my heels to the floor.

"I'm getting tired of repeating myself."

I shake my head again.

"Don't make me come get you."

Fuck. If I run will he chase me down?

He rises from the bed in one smooth movement and my fight or flight instincts kick in. Before I even realize what I'm doing, I'm spinning around, pulling open the door.

He's on top of me before I get across the threshold. There just wasn't enough space between us to give me a good head start.

Grabbing me by the hips, he yanks me back and slams the

door. There's a moment where my feet leave the floor then I'm roughly pressed up against the door, my cheek pushed against the wood.

He growls into my ear as he grinds his hips into my ass.

Fuck, I think what I did turned him on. I can feel something hard rubbing against me.

"That wasn't a very smart decision," he sighs and I feel his teeth nipping at the back of my neck.

"Please," I whine and stiffen. That nip at my neck sends a jolt of sensation straight to my core.

My mind and body are at war.

I know he's an awful despicable person, despite how kind he's been with the children, and I'm afraid this is all some sick twisted game to him.

We're only safe here until he gets bored with us or something better comes along.

"Please, what?" he asks, his breath hot against the wet spot he left on my neck.

"Please, let us go."

He grinds his hips hard into my ass and says coldly, "No."

"Why?" I cry out in despair.

His hips let up and he pulls away, and I feel this wild hope that he's going to let me go. But then he grabs me by the hips and spins me around to face him.

He pushes me back and the palms of my hands slap against the door.

He leans forward, caging me in with his arms. Head bending down, his forehead nearly touches my forehead as he stares into my eyes and says, "Because I don't want to."

Staring into his eyes is like staring into the abyss. There's a power in them that's sucking out my fight. My will.

It's becoming harder and harder to remain strong.

"You can't do this," I say weakly.

His lips curve into a smug smile. "I can."

That smugness immediately makes me bristle with pent-up anger. I need the anger, desperately. I need the fire of rage to protect my heart. "What gives you the right?"

His eyes drop to my lips. "I have the right of might. I can do anything I want."

As if to prove his point, his lips press against my lips and he kisses me hard and deep as if he's trying to devour my mouth.

His lips slant over my lips.

His tongue presses, insistent, seeking entrance.

He's so soft, his cheeks, his lips.

His tongue.

My lips give way to him and I feel myself opening up, eager to taste him.

Eager to be devoured.

He kisses me until all the resistance goes out of me, until I'm slumping against the door. My knees weaken. He kisses me until I'm breathless and clinging to his shirt.

Pulling slowly away from me, his eyes are hooded. His lips swollen and glistening.

Reaching down, he tenderly brushes the hair from my eyes and it's so tender it *hurts*.

He treats me with more care, with more affection than Marshall ever did, but he doesn't seem to care about what I want. I get no choices. I have no power.

Yet my body doesn't care.

A part of me just wants to give in. To stop fighting. To melt in his arms.

Why keep fighting? Why not just enjoy the moment? It would be so easy to live in the now and forget about tomorrow…

But I've done that before. I've ignored my better instincts.

I've let little things slide until they became big things and I no longer had any control.

And where did it get me? It got me here.

"It's not right. Don't you see that? You can't just own a person. I'm not a pet, my children and I aren't animals. You can't just claim us or act as if you own us. It's *wrong*."

Lucifer blinks at me in surprise and then frowns. His eyes harden and his voice is cold. "It is wrong... to you," he agrees, surprising me. "And I don't give a fuck. Right or wrong. Black or white. It's all in the eye of the beholder. In my world, I see something I want, I take it. I took you."

My eyes prickling with tears, I say, "That doesn't mean you can get away with this... even if you don't see what's wrong with it, doesn't mean there won't be consequences for you."

Lucifer nods his head slowly and then his finger sweeps across my cheek, gathering up a tear. He sticks the finger in his mouth and then grins down at me. "It's the way of the world, Lilith. No one is going to stop me because there is no one stronger to stop me. The strong take and the weak, well, they get taken. No one is going to come along to rescue you."

He doesn't have to say it but I feel it hanging in the air.

*Your own husband doesn't even want you.*

My tears flood my eyes, blurring my vision and I'm crying in earnest now. All of this is just too fucked up, and I've completely lost all hope of him changing his mind and deciding to let us go. He truly believes he's untouchable.

Lucifer sighs and pulls me close, cradling me in his arms. I'm weak and I need his touch, his heat. His comfort. I bury my face into his chest and cry into his shirt. One hand rubs soothingly down my back while the other tenderly pets my hair.

I can't even remember the last time someone held me like

this when I was upset. Maybe my mother did when I was little?

He lets me cry on him, he lets me soak him with my tears. Once my sobs quiet and I feel like I've gotten most of it out, he murmurs. "Don't worry, my dear. I don't want to force you, I just want to possess you."

I shudder in his arms and he sweeps me up. Spinning me around, he carries me to the bed like some gallant prince and gently lowers me down.

He's being so tender, so careful, he's making it really hard for me to continue hating him.

A pleasant numbness settles over me as he straightens.

From down here he seems larger than life, almost unreal. The way his eyes glide over my body, drinking me in, I feel desired.

Wanted.

*Oh, god, this so wrong. So wrong...*

His long, strong fingers go to the collar of his shirt and begin to slowly unbutton it. As his fingers work their way down, my body flushes with anticipation. I'm practically squirming and panting with it.

Shirt open, he yanks it out of his pants and slides it off, revealing hard, bulging biceps and a rippling chest. I knew he was strong, I could feel it when I was trapped in his arms, but I didn't realize he was packing so much muscle beneath his suit.

My eyes roam over him and now it's my time to drink him in. To burn his visage into my brain.

He's so damn beautiful, so damn perfect, I'm pretty sure I've seen sculptures of him in a museum.

Fingers latching onto his belt buckle, he flips it open and then yanks the belt hard out of his pants.

As his pants slide down to the floor, revealing his tight

black briefs and the obvious erection trapped within them, I come back to my senses.

Scrambling backward, I try to escape him but he strikes fast. Grabbing me by the ankles, he yanks me back down the bed.

"Where do you think you're going?" he asks.

Before I can even answer his weight is coming down on top of me, his mouth is crushing against my lips.

He kisses me fiercely, distracting me as his knees nudge my knees apart.

With each pull from his mouth, with each thrust of his tongue, I feel my will to fight weaken and wilt.

I want this, I realize. Even after last night, I'm starved for more.

Aching for him.

Fitting himself between my thighs, he rocks his hips forward, grinding and rubbing himself against my panties.

My core is filled with a hot, needy pressure.

A moan rises up in my throat as I lift my hips up, asking for more.

He groans in return, his kiss becoming deeper, the grinding of his hips harder. My hands find his shoulders, but instead of pushing him away, I'm gripping him, tugging on him.

Trying to bring him closer.

Suddenly he breaks away and the rocking of his hips stops. With a keening cry, my fingers tighten around him and I try to pull him back down.

He grins down at me with satisfaction and purrs, "So needy already, kitten?"

Instantly, I feel my ardor begin to cool.

He tips his head back and laughs, amused by the annoyed look on my face and then his gaze drifts down.

"As much as I want you," he says and rocks his hips forward as if to leave no doubt about it. "I want to see you. Every inch of you. It was impossible to see last night in the dark."

Panting, I turn my face to the side. The thought of him seeing me naked for some reason fills me with a new fear. What if he doesn't find me attractive? What if he thinks my body is ugly?

Fuck, why do I even care?

"Remove your dress," he commands and leans back, giving me space.

When I don't immediately jump to do his bidding he sarcastically asks, "Need help?"

I shake my head in refusal and he seems to lose all patience with me.

With a snarl he reaches down, grabs the front of my dress and pulls, snapping the threads. Yanking and ripping angrily, he splits my dress straight down the front.

My breasts spill out and all of my torso is exposed. His eyes gleam as they glaze over me, and I'm frozen. Paralyzed. I don't know what to do.

I feel painfully vulnerable at this moment.

"You're lucky I'm feeling merciful tonight," he rasps, eyes locking on the rising and falling swells of my breasts. "Tomorrow I expect you to do what you're told."

Do what I'm told?

"Fuck you." I spit out and try to push at his shoulders, to shove him away.

He laughs, grabbing me by the wrists. Pinning my arms to my sides.

"You are so fucking beautiful when you're angry," he smirks and that only pisses me off more.

I growl and buck beneath him, trying to escape his grip.

His head dips down, his hot mouth covers the peak of my breast, and I still at once.

Fuck, why does it have to feel so good?

With a groan, he pulls back a hard suckle and both of my nipples pucker and tighten into two hard little buds.

His mouth works me over, sucking, nipping, and licking my breast. Each lash of his tongue, each suck of his mouth is breaking down the last of my resistance.

There's only so much I can take, so much I can stand. I can't even remember the last time a man played with my breasts let alone sucked and worshipped them like he is.

He groans and I watch, entranced as he pulls back, allowing my dusky, glistening nipple to slide out of his mouth.

His eyes are closed and he has this look on his face like he's really enjoying what he's doing. Like I'm the best damn thing he's ever tasted. He doesn't even open his eyes to look where he's going, he just moves over to the other breast and begins to suck and lick on it like he can't get enough of it.

The empty ache inside of me keeps growing and growing until I feel like my entire body is throbbing with the force of it.

"Fuck, I love these tits," he groans, mouth releasing my breast with a wet smack.

His tongue gives my nipple one last parting long lick and then his teeth are nibbling their way down my ribs.

Breasts warm and heavy against my chest, my core tenses as he kisses and nips a wet trail down my stomach.

"What are you doing?" I ask, trying to keep the fear out of my voice.

He's not planning on doing what I think he is… is he? He can't.

He doesn't answer me. He just keeps nipping and licking

his way down until he reaches my lacy black panties. Only then do his eyes lift to regard me, piercing and intense.

"I'm going to let go of your wrists. If you fight me I'll be forced to tie you up. Do you understand?"

My throat tightens and my heart quickens with trepidation. The last thing I want is to be tied up and completely at his mercy. In fact, right now that would pretty much be my worst nightmare.

But if he tries to do something I don't want him to do how can I keep myself from trying to fight him?

His grip around my wrists eases. I flex my fingers and rotate my wrists to get the circulation flowing again.

"Place your palms flat on the bed."

"Why?" I ask without thinking and immediately regret it.

His face darkens and I slap both my hands against the bed to appease him.

"Good girl," he says and now his eyes glint with wickedness. "Keep them there until I give you permission to move them. Do you understand?"

I understand but I sure as hell don't like it.

Frowning, I nod my head.

He sighs and his head drops down, his teeth nipping at my thigh.

I yelp and jerk away from him.

"I said, do you understand?"

"Yes!"

"Good girl," he murmurs and then proceeds to kiss the spot on my thigh he just bit.

The hurt is quickly soothed and my fingers grip at the sheet as the pain melts into a more pleasurable sensation.

His mouth. God, I love his mouth. I hate him, but I love those lips of his.

I feel myself relaxing, sinking into the bed. He turns his head and there's the lightest scrape of his stubble as he goes to work on the other thigh. I'm so relaxed I spread my legs for him.

His hands slide up my legs, lingering at my stomach and then he's rolling my panties down my hips.

Instantly, I stiffen, fighting the urge to reach down and stop him. I have no doubt that if I lift my palms from this bed he'll do exactly as he promised.

He stops kissing my thigh and looks up at me, his eyes filled with triumph. My hands clench into fists. I want to smack that triumphant look off of his face.

Then the cool air hits my sex and I shiver. I didn't even realize I was so wet.

His gaze drops and he stares hard at me. Immediately, I close my legs and lock my knees.

"Don't you fucking hide from me," he growls and reaches down, pulling my legs apart.

I cry out, utterly mortified. Tears of shame blur my vision.

His gaze drops again to my exposed pussy, his fingers digging into my knees and keeping me spread.

I turn my face away, unable to watch. Seconds tick by, and I just want to crawl into a hole and die. I wish he would just get this over with.

Then his breath hits my inner thigh and I sense movement down there. I glance down in panic and sure enough he's getting up close and personal. He's sticking his face all up in my business.

"Oh my god, what are you doing?" I ask.

"What does it look like I'm doing?" he smirks. "I'm admiring the view."

My cheeks flush with heat and the burn spreads all the way down my chest. "Please don't."

"Don't what?" he asks, pretending to be confused, but that

smirk of his sharpens. "Don't look at this beautiful pink little pussy?"

"Oh god," I gasp and shake my head.

He blows his warm breath right against my clit.

The little bundle of nerves lights up and all my muscles tense. My teeth sink into my lip as I swallow back a moan.

"This is my pussy now, and I plan to fully fucking enjoy it. Do you understand?"

Before I can catch my breath, his tongue touches my folds and slowly, torturously, drags up, parting them.

"Oh shit," I gasp and my fingers claw at the bed.

I've never been licked down there before and it's way, *way* too intense.

His tongue pauses right before he reaches my clit, leaving me hanging on the edge. "Do you understand, Lily?"

Shit. Understand what?

It takes me a second to figure out what he's asking. The pulsing in my core is so strong it's driving me to distraction.

If only he could touch my clit and ease it a little bit...

"Yes," I gasp. I figure that's the answer he wants for the question he's asking.

He makes a rumbling sound of approval and then his tongue is touching me again. Another slow lap up, he takes his time as if he's truly savoring me. As if he's truly enjoying this.

Then he pauses just before my clit and I'm squirming in frustration.

*Just do it, dammit.*

"Whose pussy is this, Lily?"

"Huh?"

What's with the twenty questions?

He blows against me, and gah! It's just enough to aggravate the pulsing throb but not enough to do anything about it.

"Whose pussy is this, Lily?" he repeats and then his tongue is on me again, doing little circles around my clit.

Now I know why he's called Lucifer, because he's an evil, evil man...

"Yours," I say softly, so softly.

Fingers clutching the sheet, my back arches and my hips rock up, trying to guide his tongue to where I need it.

Growling, he grabs me by the hips firmly and pins me back down to the bed.

"You're so fucking sweet," he says huskily, the vibrations of his voice driving me crazy.

I want those little vibrations just a little higher but just as his tongue almost touches my clit he quickly licks back down.

I throw my head back and cry out in frustration.

He chuckles and repeats his question. "Whose pussy is this, Lily?"

"Yours," I grit out from between my teeth.

The tip of his tongue very lightly flicks against my clit. "Tell me."

I want to move my hips but his grip tightens on them. Tears of frustration sting my eyes. I don't want to give in to him. I don't. I don't want to yield, and I sure as hell don't want to submit, but my body is making it too difficult to resist him.

Maybe if I wasn't so sexually frustrated... Maybe if I had gotten to enjoy sex more than once a year, I'd have the strength or the fortitude to stand up to him.

But I don't.

I just don't have it.

I'm a weak, pitiful woman.

"It's yours," I whisper and it feels like I just ripped myself open.

"What is?" I hear him suck in a deep breath then he's blowing a jet of hot air directly on my clit.

"My pussy," I whine, my back arching.

"Whose pussy is this?"

"Your pussy!" I cry out and all at once I experience heaven.

His hot mouth completely covers my clit and sucks hard on it.

I'm so wet, so hot, all my bones turn to liquid.

*Yes.* I needed this. I needed this push to let go. I needed this excuse to surrender, to give up, even if it's only for a moment.

Bliss, pure bliss flows through my veins. My blood is like lava; so hot it's nearly boiling as it pumps straight to my sex.

My thighs lock around his head and he just keeps sucking and sucking. The throbbing is eased but it's replaced by the most delicious pressure. His hands grab my thighs. His fingers dig into my skin as he spreads me wide open.

He growls and makes all these deep noises in his throat as he devours me. Then out of nowhere his teeth clamp down, pinching my clit.

I explode in a gush, crying out in surrender. All the little knots inside me that keep me together release.

I'm unbound. Free from all my constrictions.

His mouth moves. Lips and tongue working me over, making wet, sucking noises as he consumes me. Eating me up. No part of me is left untouched.

He sucks on my lips and dips his tongue into my tight entrance.

My orgasm seems to go on for an eternity and I'm all warm and fuzzy as I slowly float back down to my senses.

Lucifer gives my folds one last long lick and then his head pops up. His face is wet from me but his eyes are glowing and intense.

First, his eyes go to my hands still gripping the sheet and he grins with satisfaction. My fingers are starting to cramp up now that I'm aware of them again so I release my grip on the sheet and flex them.

That satisfied grin remains on his lips as he slowly crawls up my body. And there's just something about it that causes my heart to flutter behind my ribs.

"You can move your hands now, Lily," he says, but I don't know what else to do with them.

So I keep them planted on the bed.

Positioning himself above me, he reaches down, grabs me by my hair and tips my head back. Then his mouth is crushing against my mouth and I'm tasting myself on his lips.

"Do you taste how sweet you are?" he growls against my lips and then his tongue is thrusting inside my mouth.

Stroking against my tongue. Reawakening my neediness.

As he kisses me his knees nudge at my knees, and I'm so relaxed, so fuzzy, I obediently open for him.

The hot, velvety head of his cock nudges at my entrance and I gasp against his mouth, breaking the kiss.

Fingers loosening, he pets my hair back. His eyes capture my eyes, and he stares hard at me as he reaches between us.

"Fuck, you're so wet," he sighs, rubbing his cock against me, torturing my oversensitive clit as he slicks himself up with my juices.

My eyes start to roll back into my head and his fingers are tightening in my hair again.

"Look at me, Lily," he demands, and I struggle to focus my eyes on him. "Look at me as I enter you."

He pushes forward, slowly filling me up, stretching me inch by slow inch. I'm soaking wet and swollen after my orgasm but he's so big I still feel that little pinch of resistance.

"God damn, you're tight," he says, his voice raw and his eyes strained as he buries himself deep inside me.

Bottoming out, he holds himself there, giving me a moment to adjust around him.

The hand that was helping guide his cock goes to the bed and he pushes up, gaze dropping to look between us.

Slowly, he withdraws, pulling himself out and then he slams himself back in.

My own gaze drifts down and I watch as his red, glistening cock disappears inside me. He's so damn big I don't even know how he fits.

Looking up, he catches me watching and then a mischievous grin stretches across his lips. Pulling back, he slides himself almost completely out of me and then he throws himself forward, filling me up with him.

My spine arches and this time I can't stop my eyes from rolling back in my head. I cry out and reach up, grabbing at him, needing something to hold on to. Needing something to help me get through these intense sensations.

He's so big, so thick, he's touching every dark little spot buried inside me.

"Fuck," he grunts, pulling himself out and then he slams back in.

There's no mercy, no hesitation.

Just a barrage of pleasure, an attack on my senses.

It feels so fucking good. Deep down, I know it shouldn't. I know I shouldn't give in but I'm just too weak to keep fighting it.

In and out, his velvety length glides inside me and he stares hard down at me, his eyes filled with possession.

At this point I just have to admit to myself I want this. I *need* this.

There's this great big gaping hole I've been carrying around inside me, and right now he's filling it.

"You fucking like it, don't you?" he snarls above me and his pace increases.

He's slamming himself in and out of me so hard, so fast, his skin begins to slap against my skin.

"You like me fucking you, don't you Lily?" he grunts in exertion.

*Yes*, I like him fucking me.

"You were made to take my cock," he grunts as the rocking of his hips increases. "Your little pussy was made for me to fuck. Wasn't it?"

*Yes, yes, yes.*

Reaching down, he grabs my leg by the back of my knee and pulls it up, tilting my hips. His next thrust goes even deeper and he smashes against my clit.

"Fuck you feel good," he grunts out.

He pulls back and pounds into me again.

It's too much. Too much pressure, too much sensation. I'm overwhelmed, and as his cock strokes deep inside me, finding that buried bundle of nerves, I feel myself pushed into another plane of existence.

My world begins to turn white but even through the haze, I'm aware of him snapping.

I don't know what sets it off. Maybe it's my sex gripping him, pulling him in. Maybe it's because I can't stop moaning his name and scoring my nails down his back.

"Fuck," he snarls and his face is a mask of possession mixed with aggression.

He begins to fuck me hard and fast. He begins to fuck me like he hates me.

He fucks me like I hate him.

And I do hate him. I hate him for taking me. I hate him for keeping me prisoner.

Most of all I hate him for making me feel this.

His chin drops and his icy eyes glare at me.

I'd be afraid, I'd be terrified of him if it didn't feel so good. I'm already trapped in the throes of an orgasm and it's so incredible even his madness won't ruin it.

He grabs my other leg and yanks it up. My thighs tighten around him and I lock my ankles behind his back.

"Mine," he grunts, his weight coming down on top of me, sinking me into the bed. "You're mine, dammit. Mine. Accept it."

Another wave of bliss hits me, flowing through my body. But even as I'm lost in the pleasure, I shake my head. He can force me to come, he can use my body against me, but I won't belong to him.

"Stubborn woman," he snarls and his head bends down, his teeth sinking into my neck.

I cry out and jerk beneath him as the pain hits. My walls clamp down on his cock and his teeth slide out of my flesh.

Above me, he jerks, momentarily losing his rhythm, and his head tips back.

A roar blasts past his lips and then he's driving himself into me furiously, like he's literally trying to fuck me into submission.

Inside me I can feel him swelling and growing. Filling me with a hot stickiness.

Another intense wave of pleasure sweeps me up and I drown myself in the pleasure, letting myself be swept away in it.

The orgasm seems to go on and on and I savor every little second of it.

For this short time, I can forget. For these few euphoric moments, I'm not his prisoner, I'm not his possession.

I'm simply Lilith.

Too soon I begin to reconnect with myself, my body flipping back on all my senses.

I realize something soft and gentle is touching my face

and blink up. Above me he's stroking my cheek and looking down at me with the most tender look on his face.

That look... that look undoes me. An overwhelming surge of sadness hits my heart and my throat tightens up. Why does he have to look at me like that? Why is he making it so hard for me to hate him?

I burst into tears, hating myself because I'm weak. I'm fucking pathetic. Hating that I allowed him to make me feel all the good things I just experienced.

11

LUCIFER

*A*cceptance is the first step in understanding your new reality. Acceptance that nothing in this world or the next will ever be the same. To me, last night the clear tears streaming down her cheeks at the end were of acceptance.

Lying to myself about where I stand in things is not my style. I know Lilith will push things again, I know she will test me and herself. It's in human nature. I just plan to be the rock she crashes against when she does.

"Lucifer, we have an issue," Simon says to me as he knocks once on the door frame of the office I am sitting in.

Leaning back in my office chair, I can feel my mouth turning down in a frown. With Simon, it's never a good thing if he says we have an issue. He knows me, he knows to handle things unless they absolutely need my attention.

"I've been making calls and sending out feelers on the

missing five million," he says as he enters the office and shuts the door.

"What have you got?"

"It's the same bullshit we've known for a while. O'Riley and Marshall got together for a new business venture. The new information is that it was to start a pipeline through the Midwest with coke and heroin. They had the Yakuza as their main suppliers."

"Well that... how the fuck did that go wrong?" I ask. The Yakuza, in my experience, are deadly as fuck, but also pretty damn reliable. They promise something, it will happen. They deliver on the promise, no excuses.

"Looks like O'Riley fucked up. We don't know the full details, but the Irish took an Italian boss, Carcinelly, out. Then they took out O'Riley, the boss who ordered the hit on the Italians... It's a fucking mess over in Ohio right now. No boss for the Irish, a new one for the Italians, and hitmen running loose."

"Fuck," I mumble as I rub my temples slowly. Shit like that gives me ulcers. I don't let destabilization like that shit happen around here. It breeds too much uncertainty. And I want to be damn sure of my business deals.

"So the Irish have my money?" I ask with a grimace; those fucks are just as crazy as the Russians. Especially the hitmen they use. As of now we don't have an Irish mob around here, I like that. Having a Russian one is enough batshit nutcases for me.

"No," Simon says with a frown.

"No? Well, who has my five fucking million dollars then?"

"The Yakuza."

"Shit, how do we know?"

"Because they took it during the war up there. Even bragged about it to those around them—least that's what I am hearing. It seems like they are trying to make sure they haven't lost any face on the issue. Still could be Marshall though." Simon says, and I don't doubt a word he has said to me.

Simon is my right hand for this exact reason, he has a nose for things. The man is like a bloodhound dog, he doesn't stop tracking a scent until he has it up a tree.

"Do they know it's my money?" I ask as I think about Marshall and how fucked up of a position he has me in.

"I'm not sure of that yet, but I am making small waves around the pond to see what comes up."

"Where is Marshall so far with everything?"

"Drunk. Fall down, passing out drunk in his shitty little world of self-appreciation. Seems he is bragging to a few people about how he pulled one over on you. He's been drinking and whoring for the last twenty-four hours."

"With what money?" I ask with a growl.

"Credit cards and whatever he has in the banks."

"Get his accounts closed or frozen, I want him as broke as possible by tomorrow morning."

"Got it. What do you want me to do with the connection to O'Riley?"

I ponder that for a long moment. I know I can go to the Irish for restitution but they will more than likely play dumb on the whole situation. The question for me is do I want to go stirring the pot with them or with the Yakuza?

"Do the same thing for both the Yakuza and the Irish. Try the Italians as well. If nothing comes of them knowing it was my money that was lost, see if we can set up a meet. Do not come off as a beggar, Simon. Let them know we expect answers to the questions we have."

"Matthew, I don't think we can afford a war on those fronts," he says as he looks at me. He isn't afraid to use my birth name with me, but he knows to only do it when he has to.

"There won't be one. Right now, I want more information on what exactly happened to the money and the drugs that it bought."

"And the Irish?"

"Let's see what happens there. I'm not going over to Ohio to start a war with those fucks when I have two other ones on my front here. I want you to keep a watch out, though. If they have problems, we might be able to work our way into some new territory."

Simon nods his head and then heads out of the office, shutting the door behind him.

Turning away from my desk, I look out the corner office window to the sprawling city below me.

The Irish will play up the dumb card, then more than likely tell me to fuck off in a polite way.

The Yakuza, if they do have the money, will tell me it's my loss their gain. I can't see either giving back what's mine.

My left hand lifts and I stare at the emerald pinky ring I am wearing. It's the only thing I have left of my father that I haven't changed. When the stroke took his body and the ability to function away from him, I took over the day to day operations of all his enterprises.

He'd more than likely go to war over all of this.

He was a complete fucking fool with how he ran his businesses. He truly thought he could run them the old school way forever—always hiding in the shadows of one shady business or another.

I couldn't deal with his small frame of mind. He wanted to keep all of his people controlled, he would never allow us the chance to branch out, to do new and better things.

We were fucking stuck in the dark ages of thought and freedom.

What a stupid fuck. Putting the pillow to his face ended so many exasperating headaches.

I brought us into the dawn of a new age. We dropped all the shackles that held us back for far too long. I introduced so many things to our operations that a lot of the old men feared me out of ignorance. Those fucks are all dead and buried now, and so will be any asshole that tries to get in my way.

Out of all the plain, stupid ones, Father had one brilliant idea—he sent me to school to get an education in business. My education allowed me to see new and better ways to operate. It gave me the knowledge of how to remain a criminal but get away with it. Fuck, all corporations operate in the gray and black at one time or other, they just don't admit it.

The best thing I ever did was put a retainer on the top legal defense law firms in the nation. I have no desire to ever spend any time in jail much less prison. So, going to war and killing a bunch of turds doesn't exactly appeal to me right now.

Smirking, I remember one of my business lectures talking about mergers, takeovers and hostile takeovers.

Turning back to my desk, I dial Simon's cell phone.

"Lucifer, what's going on?"

"Have someone consider all the properties and businesses we can find that are run by the Italians and the Japanese. I want as much information as we can get on them."

"Yes, sir."

Disconnecting the call, I look down at the photo on my desk. I took it from the collection Lilith had at her home. It has her and the children all smiling in the photo, looking so happy.

No prison time for me, it would ruin my plans with her. If anyone or anything try to come between me and her, they will die a very violent death.

Government or gang thug, makes no difference to me.

## 12

LILY

*I* wake up to the first rays of the morning light streaming through the curtains and Lucifer bending over me, kissing me on the cheek.

"The nanny will be arriving later this morning," he says softly, his minty breath cool against the spot he just kissed.

I blink sleepily up at him, reluctantly leaving my dreams where I was warm, safe, and happy.

All at once awareness hits me and I remember where I am.

I remember what happened last night. What we did.

He held me in his arms and I must have cried myself to sleep.

Suddenly modest, I yank the sheets up my naked body and croak out, "Nanny?"

Nodding his head slowly, he straightens and stares down at me. He's already dressed for the day in his impeccable black suit and he smells clean, like soap.

I feel... lowly as he towers over me in the dim light. He seems even more intimidating today after everything we did last night. He knows I'm weak to him and he's empowered by it.

"Yes, I've hired a nanny to help you."

"I don't need a nanny," I immediately protest and begin to sit up, clutching the sheet to my chest.

"Regardless," he smirks. "She'll be arriving around eleven."

I hate it when he talks like that. The way he says it leaves no room to question him. "Have a good day, Lilith. I'll see you at dinner."

His eyes search my face as if he's expecting me to say or do something but I just stare at him, unsure if I should let this nanny thing slide or make a stink about it.

Maybe having a nanny around won't be such a bad thing... it could give me more time to figure a way out of this. On the other hand, though, she's another pair of eyes to keep watch on me and the children.

Nodding, Lucifer shoves his hands into his pockets and turns on his heel. He's striding out of the room when I call out to him, "Lucifer?"

Immediately he comes to a stop and turns around, almost as if he was expecting me to call out to him. "Yes?"

"May I have my phone back?" I ask hopefully. I'm completely isolated without it, disconnected from the outside world. And maybe, hopefully, after last night, he trusts me a little bit.

"No," he answers coldly, and turns on his heel.

I'm so shocked I watch him walk out of the room without stopping him.

∼

After my morning shower, I'm half tempted to throw on a

pair of sweatpants and a dirty old t-shirt just to spite him, but decide I'm more likely to get what I want if I try to please him. Maybe if I make an effort he'll reward me for it.

After having that thought I immediately feel a little sick.

This entire situation is so fucked up, and after what we did last night I'm having an even harder time trying to come to terms with it. I don't know what I want.

Do I want out of here? Do I truly want to escape? Or do I want to stay… even if it requires me to be something he owns. Another possession to add to his collection.

If he was mean, if he hurt me, or threatened my children, it would be such an easy decision. It would be so easy to hate him.

But he's not.

If anything, sadly, he's shown more interest in us, *done* more for us in a mere twenty-four hours than Marshall ever did.

He's shown me more kindness, care, and affection than the man I chose to marry ever has. How fucked up is that?

It's almost worth trading away my free will for… almost. Unfortunately, I don't think I'll ever be happy being kept like I'm a pet.

I dig through the boxes of clothes I still haven't hung up, searching for something that shows that I'm putting in a bit of effort but doesn't scream I'm trying too hard. I end up settling on a cream sweater dress and pair it with my favorite brown riding boots.

I curl my hair and slap on some makeup. I have to admit to myself it feels good to be dressed up for the day. I don't feel like I need to hide behind my sunglasses.

Waking up the children, I help them get dressed then lead them downstairs for breakfast. The cook has a complete spread of pancakes, bacon, sausage, and fruit waiting for us. We sit down together in the dining room and dig in.

Evelyn seems especially sunny today, bouncing in her seat and happily nibbling on bacon.

"How did you sleep last night?" I ask her.

"Great!" she smiles at me.

Whenever she smiles at me I can't help but smile back. Regardless of how bad things are, or what kind of stresses I have hanging over my head, her bright smiles make everything worth it.

Adam, on the other hand, is unusually quiet. He just pokes at his food, not eating much.

"How did you sleep last night, Adam?" I ask him.

He shrugs his shoulders without looking up at me.

Just as I'm about to ask Adam what's bothering him, Peter strides into the dining room and informs us it's time to leave for school. Standing from the table, we gather up their bags and lunches and head out to the car.

Stepping outside and seeing the guarded gate at the end of the long driveway just drives home how much this place feels like a prison. Peter opens up the back passenger side door for us and the children obediently climb in.

I have the quick, sickening thought that I'm teaching them this is normal. I'm teaching them that I'm okay with this.

Noticing the look on my face, Peter lifts both of his brows at me. "Is something wrong?"

How do I even explain it? Would he even care if I did?

Pressing my lips together, I shake my head and slide in after the children.

∼

AFTER DROPPING the children off at their schools, Peter immediately drives me back to the house.

With no housework to do and no way to catch up on my social media, I have nothing else to do but unpack.

Unpacking though feels like giving in. It feels like I'm accepting this.

I dig out more of the children's essentials and leave the rest sitting in the boxes.

The nanny arrives exactly at eleven o'clock, just like he said she would, and I'm relieved to find she's a sweet, older woman. She's very polite when she introduces herself as Mary and I place her in her mid to late fifties with her gray hair and dated clothing.

Awkwardly, I'm not sure how to introduce myself in return so I simply give her my name and hope she doesn't inquire further about this situation. Thankfully, she doesn't refer to me as Lucifer's wife, nor does she seem to imply that he's the father of the children.

I honestly don't know how I'd respond if she assumed that.

I show her to the children's rooms, their things, and go over our routine. She takes it all in with a smile on her face and when I'm done, I have the craziest urge to tell her the truth.

How will she react if I confess we're being held prisoner against our will? Will she offer assistance? Or will she go running to Lucifer to tell him?

I have to assume everyone he's hired he's thoroughly vetted and they're loyal to him. But what if she's not? She seems too kind, too old to be in cahoots with the likes of him.

As we're walking out of Adam's room and I'm shutting the door quietly behind us, I ask casually, "So how long have you been a nanny?"

Mary smiles at me and her gray eyes twinkle with amusement. "For more than thirty years, dear. I was Matthew's nanny when he was a boy."

I almost ask her who Matthew is but then catch myself. Isn't that what Lucifer told Adam his name was yesterday, when we were in the kitchen?

Of course he'd hire his childhood nanny. So much for appearances. If this woman helped raise him she must be half as evil as he is.

And now she's going to be taking care of my children.

"Something wrong?" she asks, reaching over to pat me on the arm, still acting sweet.

I bet she's a wolf in sheep's clothing.

I shake my head, clearing the thoughts from my head and force a smile to my lips. "I'm sorry, I just can't believe you were Matthew's nanny. You look so young."

She laughs and looks genuinely pleased by my compliment. "Ah, well he's not quite that old, and I was quite young when I was hired."

"Oh?" I ask as we make our way downstairs.

She nods her head and gets a wistful look in her eyes. "Yes. I was in my early twenties when I was hired by his father."

"What was Lu... I mean Matthew like when he was a boy?"

"Oh, he was a very serious boy. Even back then he was taking an interest in the family business."

"I'm sorry." I stop and turn to her as we reach the bottom of the stairs. "I'm afraid I've forgotten. What exactly is the family business?" I ask.

What are American gangsters calling it these days?

She gives me a look like I'm stupid and I should already know this. Patting me on the hand again, like one does with a child, she says, "Acquisitions."

# 13

LILY

When it's time to pick the children up for school Mary insists on accompanying me to learn the routine. Perhaps I'm turning into a paranoid, overly suspicious person, but I'm afraid that this is something she means to take over from me. My only two trips out of the house on a daily basis.

We pick up Adam first and of course he's cold towards Mary in the beginning but she seems unfazed by it. She doesn't try to force or coax him into conversation and eventually he warms to her. Posing at her several questions in curiosity.

Evelyn, as to be expected, is delighted to have a new friend, and spends the rest of the car drive home regaling Mary about her day at school and all the exciting adventures she had.

Once we return to the house, Mary takes over just as I

feared, and I'm left with nothing to do as she sees to the children.

With nothing else to do, I float in and out of the kitchen, checking on Rosa and dinner's progress. When I start trying to help set the table for dinner, Rosa chases me away, flapping a dish towel at me and speaking rapidly in Italian

Bored and depressed, I return to my room and begin to unpack my boxes. I'm hanging up some of my clothes in Lucifer's closet when I sense someone behind me.

Freezing in place, I stiffen as two arms wrap around me from behind then Lucifer's face is nuzzling into my neck.

He sucks in a deep breath, breathing me in. At the same time, I feel all the tension go out of him, his body deflates. Relaxing, he melds against my back.

Brushing my hair over my shoulder, his breath is warm against my ear as he asks, "How was your day?"

Horrible. Awful.

"Boring," I sigh and stretch up to hang the silk blouse in my hand.

Lucifer takes this as an opportunity to roam his hands up and over my breasts. As I lower back down to the floor, his hands cover my breasts completely, cupping them in his big hands.

My traitorous body responds instantly, flushing with heat and my nipples tightening.

"So was mine," he purrs and his teeth nip at my earlobe. "I couldn't stop thinking about you all day."

I swallow back my moan and try to fight my reaction to him. I will my blood to cool, for my breasts not to be so sensitive.

*Think of awful things. Horrible things.*

His tongue licks at my lobe and then his lips are kissing down my neck.

*Think of how awful he is; not how sexy he is.*

I try but I keep failing.

"I couldn't stop thinking about these tits."

He squeezes my breasts hard in his hands. My toes curl against the floor and I have to fight the urge to arch my back.

"Fuck, you have amazing tits," he pants and then something hard is grinding into my ass.

Oh god, why do I have to like this? Why is this making me wet? What is wrong with me?

His fingers find my nipples through my bra and they pinch.

I hate how I'm responding to him. I hate how my hips rock back and my core clenches.

"And this ass. I love your juicy little ass."

I hate how my skin breaks out in gooseflesh. I hate how my heart quickens.

One hand leaves my breast and slowly slides down my stomach. "Did you think about me, Lilith?" he asks.

"No," I grit out from between my teeth. I've only been trapped in the house all day; how could I not think about him?

He laughs and his hand slides lower and lower. Fingers pausing on top of my mons, he growls. "I couldn't stop thinking about your pink little pussy and how good you taste."

Grabbing the bottom of my dress, he yanks it up.

"What are you doing?" I gasp as the cool air hits my ass.

He shoves me forward and I throw out my hands to stop myself from crashing into the wall. Bracing myself, he kicks at my feet, forcing me to spread for him.

I cast a panicked look over my shoulder. "Lucifer?"

His eyes gleam at me and he steps forward, unbuckling his pants and tearing them open.

"Stay just like that," he commands, and I have this deep, visceral desire to obey him.

I shouldn't just stand here and let him get away with this.

And I shouldn't be panting in anticipation.

But I just can't help it. He drives me freaking crazy.

This man, he is my weakness. He is my kryptonite. I'm drawn to him. Like the moth to the flame.

He's going to burn me and consume me.

Inside I know he's going to hurt me, but there's something wrong with my wiring. I don't even try to escape.

He steps up to me, into me, and the first thing I feel is his heat against my ass. He's so warm, so velvety, I shiver. He's so hard I can feel him pulsing against my flesh.

Reaching between my spread thighs from the front, his fingers push aside my panties and slide through my lips. "Fuck, you're soaking wet," he exclaims as if he's surprised by this and then he groans, once more his mouth finding my neck.

*Oh god*, I realize I am. I'm soaked with my desire for him. What is wrong with me? Why am I so sick?

Why can't I stop wanting him?

His fingers grab onto my panties and then yank, tearing them in half.

"Fucking hell, Lily," he growls into my ear. "I can't wait. I need to be inside you *now*."

Pushing into me, there's pressure at my entrance and then he's filling me up, stretching me to my very seams.

God, he's so thick. I feel incredibly full of him.

He stills, giving me a moment to adjust around him. If he didn't, if he tried to have his way with me right now, I just know he'd break me.

His fingers move between me and the wall, the rough tips brushing against my clit. Inside I clench down on his cock, my pussy trying to pull him in deeper.

"So responsive," he says with husky appreciation.

His fingers begin to rub my clit in slow, little circles and I bite my lip to keep from crying out.

"Why do you fight it, Lilith?"

The pace of his fingers quickens and my walls are pulsing around him.

"What's the harm in giving in?"

My muscles tighten and all the little nerves in my body light up with awareness.

He hasn't even moved his cock yet but *fuck* if I'm not going to come like this.

"You belong to *me*," His teeth find my neck and he's biting me just as the first wave of my orgasm hits, rocking through my body.

As the walls of my sex pulse and spasm around him, he withdraws only to slam back inside me.

He fucks me hard and fast. Grunting and growling into my ear as he has his way with me.

He tells me how beautiful I am, and how much I make him crazy.

He tells me how frustrating I am, and how he'll kill anyone who fucks with me.

But most of all he tells me I can never get away, and he'll hunt me to the ends of the earth if I try to run away.

Body driving into my body, the world in front of my eyes goes white. I explode into the most powerful orgasm I've ever experienced in my life and his deep, throaty groan tells me he's not far behind me.

All at once I feel him swell inside me, pulsing, throbbing. My pussy locks up around him and I become trapped in the throes of my own release.

"Fuck, Lily," he roars out. "Fuck, fuck, fuck."

His hips rock forward, pumping me full of warmth as he grinds himself hard and deep.

After several long minutes, his hips gradually slow until he stills completely against me.

Panting against the back of my neck, we both catch our breath and I will my mind to remain blank.

Don't think too much about what just happened, just enjoy it.

It's done. You can't take it back.

But even now his words haunt me.

"You can never get away."

As his breath hits the back of my neck I realize he just said that out loud, it's not something repeating in my brain.

"Do you understand that, Lilith?"

When I don't answer, he twists me around to face him. "Lilith?"

Slowly, I nod my head and somehow keep the tears at bay.

Pulling me close, he kisses me long and deep.

"Once I can trust you, your life will become infinitely easier," he says as he breaks the kiss.

"Oh?" I ask, my sad, desolate little heart fluttering with hope.

"Yes," he sighs and yanks his pants up, buckling them. "You'll have more freedom to do the things that you want."

I think on his words as he takes me by the hand and leads me to the bathroom. Once we're inside, he closes the door behind us and then grabs me and lifts me up, sitting me down on the counter beside the sink.

I watch him curiously as he walks over to the shower and grabs a rag. Returning, he orders me to, "Lift your skirt."

"Why?" I ask, eyeing the rag.

"I want to wash you."

Cheeks flaming with heat, I hesitate.

"Do it or I'll do it for you, Lilith," he growls. "And you won't like it my way."

He just fucked me silly, yet pulling my skirt up for him to clean me still feels utterly humiliating. He sighs as I hold the skirt up at my waist and takes a step forward.

"Spread your legs."

Tipping my head up, I stare up at the ceiling and obey.

Behind me, I hear the faucet turn on and then a bottle opening.

"Why did you hire your childhood nanny?" I ask while I wait for him to touch me with the rag.

The faucet turns off and then there's a gush of water. He must be squeezing out the rag. "Because I want you and the children to have everything you need."

The rag drips all over my thighs before it touches me. I'm still so sensitive, I groan as he rubs the wet fabric against my tender pussy.

"Thank you," I grit out slowly and drop my chin, tearing my gaze away from the ceiling. "I appreciate it, I do."

"You're welcome," he grins down at me and pulls back the rag.

Leaning around me, he turns the faucet back on and rinses the rag out in the sink.

"I don't want to come off as ungrateful, though, but now I have nothing to do all day."

Turning off the water, he squeezes out the rag then leaves it sitting beside the sink. Grabbing a small, fluffy hand towel, he turns back to me and begins to dry my thighs.

"There are other things you could do."

"Like what?" I ask, trying to keep the frustration out of my voice. "I can't cook, or clean, or do my own laundry…"

Frowning, he finishes drying me then pulls my skirt out of my hands and smooths it down my thighs for me. Taking a step back, he reaches into his back pocket and pulls out his wallet. Selecting a black card out of his wallet, he holds it out to me.

I eye the card, then I eye his face. Is this a test? Is he teasing me?

"Here, take it," he says thrusting the card at me.

Plucking the card from his fingers, I say tentatively, "Thank you?"

"If you're bored, just ask Peter to take you out during the day. As long as you have an escort, I have no problem with you leaving the grounds as long as you promise me you won't try to run away."

Clutching the card to my chest like it's my lifeline, I'm quick to promise him, "I won't run away."

"Good," he smiles taking me at my word instantly, and maybe it's my good mood or maybe it's his good mood but that smile lights up his beautiful face. "The matter is settled. Now you have something to do all day."

He takes a step toward me and I find myself eagerly spreading my legs. As he leans down towards me, my eyes are immediately drawn to his lips. My own lips tingle with the anticipation that he's going to kiss me

"What's my limit?" I ask before we get too carried away.

That smile of his twists into a mischievous grin. "I don't know. Why don't you show me?"

## 14

LUCIFER

Slipping out of the bed, I stand to stretch out my back. It was another good night sleeping next to Lilith. She may still try to show her independence from me during the day, but at night, in her sleep, she clings to my body as if I am the warm hearthstone in a blizzard. Her legs wrap tightly over mine as she clings to my chest.

It's an act of pure attrition to get out of bed without burying myself between her luscious thighs.

Dressing myself after the shower, I pull a phone from the pocket of the suit I wore last night.

"Lilith."

"Mmph," she grumbles from where she has her head buried deep in the pillow.

"Lilith, I have something for you," I say as I pull her hand up from the bed. Slipping the smartphone in her hand, I lean over and kiss the back of her head.

Then, as she shifts herself from beneath the covers, I see a delicious ass clad in only panties bare itself. Slapping the meaty part of her rump, I smile.

God that ass turns me on.

Quickly flipping over, she glares at me. There's a fire in her eyes that makes my cock ache with need to consume her again right this second.

"What, you don't like the phone?" I ask.

Sitting up, she peppers me with questions. It's not the normal smartphone that she is use to, this one is far more powerful and secure. I can't afford for her to accidentally mess up and let anything slip.

~

"How's Marshall doing?" I ask Simon after I get into the car.

Today is going to be a long day in the city. I want it to be over with as fast as I can. I have things at home I much rather be doing or fucking.

"Pissed off enough that he has started to call in the favors he's owed in some of the circles he floats."

"You said trying, he's not been successful?" I ask.

"Nope. I bought out anyone who might owe him something. I have also bought out any debt he has with any of the other families. Any bank he could have tried getting a loan from now sees his credit rating in the low 400's. Payday loan places won't even touch him. There isn't a single person or institution who would take a chance on him."

Chuckling, I look out the window at the white covered world surrounding us. Simon is a master at destroying someone. I have no clue where he got the contacts he has, but they are many and in all branches of the world.

"Have his gas turned off," I say.

Looking back at me, Simon smirks. "Already did that this morning."

"Christ, you're a cruel fuck."

"It's why you pay me."

"Where are we with the strip club?" It's only been a couple of weeks but I want to get all of this business over with before Christmas happens. We need holiday income and traffic to gather a momentum.

The holidays are almost over and they are my big times of the year. It's like Black Friday for me.

Strip clubs are a steady stream of income most of the year, but the holidays have huge spikes. Loners, college students, and business fucks all come to here, seeking something, and I make sure they feel at home. Valentine's day will be the last big spike for a while.

Big spenders put money into my business which puts money into my pockets. With the way Lilith uses my card I need that money.

Well, not really, she isn't even denting my outer layer of money but she sure did try that first week. I think she expected me to raise some concern after she went shopping those first couple of days. Clothes for her and the children were the first things she bought, though, of course she bought more for them. Coats and boots, snow pants and gloves. She has the two completely set for the next three winters.

Electronics, new bed sets. Toys.

This morning, though, I think she was trying to get a reaction out of me when she talked about adding an addition to the house and potentially adding an inground pool. When I told her to talk to Peter about who to get bids from she fell back in bed with a hand over her eyes and a quiet growl rolling off her lips.

I can break someone in more than one way.

These past two weeks have given me a reason to push harder on Marshall. I want his stupid, fuck ass broken. I want him so fucked up he dies off in some miserable gutter.

I'm happy with my new family, ready-made as it is.

I have a woman I can barely control my baser instincts around, two small children who are becoming... A welcome intrusion? I'm not use to having someone besides an occasional companion in my home. But the two little living, thinking, sentient beings are growing on me.

I had no clue they would do or say the things they do. I never knew that a female could reach that high of an octave in a screech. I think Evie, as she told me she wants to be called, broke some of the glassware. She is the constant source of happiness in the house. Now that she is comfortable, she knows no stranger and is fearless when it comes to doing anything she wants.

I do feel sorry for Peter though; it seems he is the one sought out for tea times and makeup parties. More than once I have had to send him off to home because his nails were pink. How can a man go about collecting and taking someone out when he has bright pink fingernails?

Then there is Adam, he is so serious and observant. I've no doubt he is aware of far more than either Lilith or I give him credit. His intelligence is off the charts. I'm often proud of his logic when we discuss some of our business issues. He is certainly going to be an asset as he gets older and takes on more of the business. He may be a touch ruthless, but that comes from me. I have shown him a few good ways to get results out of those around us.

The first time we talked in our office, I had him sit across from my desk. Without any hesitation, he told me that if it's our office then he must have a desk in there as well. I still chuckle over how happy he was when I told him I agreed. Now he goes there every day after school to do his school work. His poor mother and nanny, though, must never enter lest they are called for. It is our office after all.

"Good, the inspection yesterday went off without a hitch. I have the money transferring to his account today. We won't have any issues with getting the licenses transferred to us, either."

"Excellent. Any word on the money?"

"The Irish have told us it wasn't their problem, especially since one of their own was murdered. They have a bounty for the killer, but it's mostly for show, I think, because of who did the job and the fact that he has gone completely off the radar."

I am not surprised by this.

"The Yakuza have flat out refused to return any of the money much less speak with us about the missing cash. That's stupid but not something I can justify going to war over yet. They're willing to meet up, but are keeping it at a distance. If we have a business venture they will hear us out, otherwise we are being told the same thing as the Irish. Go fuck ourselves."

The Yakuza's assets are interesting, just like the Italians. Both are carefully carving out new territories for themselves, but with the Russians and I already firmly planted in place in Garden City, there isn't much for them to snap up except for our table scraps.

Neither outfit is going to be satisfied with what's left. So my bet is they will fuck with each other before taking on one of the two powerhouses.

Then again, when it comes to money and power you never know.

How they will attack each other though will be interesting. The Yakuza are known for their takeover abilities with businesses and corporations. Blackmail being a fine art for them. The Italians should never be counted out though.

They are modern and have a way of never forgetting a grudge.

"They want to meet up in a week, somewhere neutral."

"Why the fuck do they want it on neutral ground? I haven't made a single threat on them yet."

"They are weary of your dealings in the past with anyone who might have crossed you, is my thinking."

"They have, to an extent. Unknowingly, but they have, Simon. To act like they have is…" I growl but shake my head before I finish.

"They know that too, but they will not be willing to lose face over the matter. They think they are in the right despite what they did."

"Fine. Set the meeting up. We will see how they respond to me meeting with the Italians first."

"When did I set up that meeting?" he asks.

"Right now."

"Got it."

Fucking shit dicks. They want to act like big men, let's see how they like seeing me with another lover.

"Anything new with Bart?" I ask.

"Nothing, all's quiet on that front. One thing, though, is his mother is dying from some form of cancer. They found out the results about a day ago."

"Hmph… Have all the bills taken care of. Make sure she is in the best care."

THE DAY GOES SO SLOWLY that I can feel my life slowly draining out of me. If I still had any piece of my soul left I am sure today would wipe it out. There hasn't been anything but the dull life of a businessman putting out fires from one company to the next.

Rubbing my temples, I frown at the thought of doing this for another hour.

If Adam were old enough to have some formal education behind him, I would have his ass here doing this shit. Let him go gray working with the fucking staffing issues, figuring out all types of shit that has nothing to do with being a damn criminal.

"Fuck it."

Pushing the button on my desk phone, I say, "Melissa, I'm done for the day. Have Andrew meet me with the car."

Her voice comes through the phone sultry. "Yes, sir. Will there be anything I can do for you?"

She's been on the prowl again lately, trying to get to the thick cock in my pants. Not going to happen though. I have a woman back home to keep me more than interested.

Melissa is a trophy wife type, she just wants to sit and look pretty all day. To command all the servants to do her bidding. Boring and plain. She would no doubt bear children for me, but then insist on plastic surgery to fix what childbirth can do to a woman. She'd never put the effort in like Lilith does.

I dial Lilith's phone and hear the hint of annoyance in her voice. "Yes? Did you have to make this thing so complicated to use?"

"It's for your safety, dear. We're going out tonight and I want you to dress up to impress me. Make sure you show off those legs."

I don't let her say anything else as I disconnect from the call. That should get her nice and riled up for me.

I want to hit the new club tonight. The changes I had the owner start making should be showing by now. No more backroom fucking for drugs, and the crackhead strippers are gone. It's also the right time to make a call out to the Italians to see how they are feeling.

Calling up Simon, I say, "Have you set anything up with the Italians yet?"

"Not yet, something come up?"

"Yeah, see if you can get them to come to the new club tonight. We can have drinks and talk about a few things."

"Fuck. Is this *we*, as in you and me, or *we* as in something else?" he grouses at me.

Fucker can't even go to a strip club. He's a gigantic germaphobe.

"You, Lilith and I."

"Are you serious?"

I disconnect the call before laughing out loud.

## 15

LILY

*I* think I've been drunk on sex. The past two weeks have gone by in a haze of orgasms and ecstasy. I was deprived for so long I feel like I've been overdosing on endorphins, and it's seriously impacting my decision making capabilities.

I've spent my nights in bed with Lucifer, and I've spent my days shopping, pushing his credit limit.

There could be worse ways to live, I suppose, but I'm seriously beginning to question my sanity.

Seriously, what the fuck am I doing? Am I just going to accept this situation? Am I literally just going to lie down and take it?

Whenever I'm in Lucifer's presence, it's so much harder to remember that I hate him. So much harder to remember that I resent him for stripping me of my freedom.

I should hate and resent him, shouldn't I? I shouldn't just accept this…

He should respect me as a person. He should consider that I have feelings, and desires, and dreams. That I'm not just something he can keep locked away in his house. I'm not some toy he can refuse to share with the world.

This is no way to live.

Is it?

But each day it's getting harder to remember why I'm harboring such anger for him. I'm adjusting to my situation, adapting to the unusual circumstances.

And so are the children.

Adam, I've never seen him so happy or so relaxed. The tenseness he's always carried around in his little shoulders is gone. I didn't realize it before, but I think being 'the man of the house' all those days Marshall was off fucking his mistresses put a lot of pressure on him.

I feel like the shittiest of mothers for allowing him to suffer that. Now that Lucifer is around I can tell Adam looks up to him. He trusts him with the burden of responsibility he took on his little self.

And Evelyn, she's as bubbly as ever. Even more so now that she has so many people around to give her their time and attention. If it's one thing in the world she loves it's attention.

Should I even try to take them away from this? It truly seems like Lucifer has given them more than he has taken.

I suppose it's all a matter of ethics and morality. Where do I draw the line? How far am I willing to push my own principles for my family's benefit?

After all, I'm still technically a married woman. No papers have been drawn up, no lawyers have been contacted as far as I know. Lucifer has never mentioned it.

I worry that he's doing this all out of revenge.

When he's done, when's he rubbed it in all the appropriate faces, will he drop us like a bad habit?

Why am I even worried about it? *Why?* I should look forward to it, dammit. I shouldn't be *afraid* of losing him...

Speaking of revenge, is there such a thing as revenge shopping? Because if there is then I've been doing a lot of it. I've done more frivolous shopping in the past two weeks than I've done in the past two years combined. I have so many new dresses and shoes, I'm starting to push Lucifer out of his own closet.

And he doesn't seem to care. It's infuriating, but I suppose it's to be expected. Very little seems to affect him. The only time I see him get worked up is right before he's yanking down his pants and thrusting inside me. That's when I get to watch the mask slip to the side to reveal the real man.

The man that hungers, the man that's possessive.

The man that's weak to me, who has to remind me not to leave him...

When I get the call that he wants to take me out tonight, my pathetic little heart jumps in excitement.

Is he taking me out on a date? Perhaps he's going to court me in the proper fashion?

I spend the rest of the day trying on my new dresses and doing my hair and makeup. I change my mind at least a dozen times and go through dress after dress before finally settling on a classic—a little black cocktail dress that's so short it's almost indecent. The dress hits me above my midthigh and the flared skirt flashes a bit of my panties if I bend over. Paired with stiletto heels and a sequined clutch, I feel beautiful and elegant.

I can't even remember the last time I dressed up like this, and I'm hoping I'm not overdressed. I'm hoping he takes me out to somewhere fancy and elegant.

When the car pulls up to the house, it's an exercise of self-control to keep myself from running up to it in excitement. I force myself to wait patiently for Simon to open the back door for me but I can't keep my lips from smiling.

Climbing into the backseat takes some more care than usual. I have to be careful not to flash my panties to the world. But once I'm seated next to Lucifer, his reaction makes it all worth it. His eyes light up with heat before the door is even closed and he reaches over, pulling me onto his lap.

"You look beautiful," he purrs and nuzzles his face into my neck.

"Thank you, but please don't mess up my hair. I've spent all day curling it and pinning it."

"Mmm," he rumbles and his warm palm touches down on my thigh. Slowly he drags his hand up, and I fight the urge to spread for him. "I like that. You've spent all day making yourself beautiful for me."

His teeth graze down my neck, nipping at my shoulder.

I shiver, little goosebumps breaking out across my skin. "Yes, I've spent all day getting ready. I've really been looking forward to this."

"So have I," he growls and his fingers push between my thighs, forcing me to open for him. "I've been thinking about your legs all day. Thinking about doing this..."

Just as his hand pushes up my skirt and his fingers are pushing aside my panties the car comes to a stop.

"Are we here?" Lucifer asks Simon gruffly.

He curses when Simon responds, "Yes."

I sigh with disappointment as he pulls his hand out and smooths down my skirt. I was really looking forward to him getting me off, it would make getting through dinner so much easier.

Simon's door opens and shuts. A moment later our back-door is being opened. I feel Lucifer's hand against my ass as I climb out of the car, and then he's behind me, pulling down my skirt.

Straightening, I give myself a once over and decide to adjust my dress a bit. Lucifer's hand touches the small of my back and he's leading me forward before I even have a chance to look at the place.

Dress back in place, I glance up and then frown in confusion. The building is ugly, made of dark stone and windowless. There's a single steel security door serving as the side entrance and a beefy bouncer stands in front of it.

Above the door is a neon pink sign that reads: Lucky's Tails.

What kind of restaurant is this?

"Evening, boss," the bouncer nods at Lucifer and doesn't even look at me, keeping his eyes purposely averted. He steps to the side as we approach, allowing us to pass.

As soon as we step inside and the door slams behind us, I dig in my stiletto heels and turn on Lucifer.

"You brought me to a strip club?!" I hiss in indignation above the fading chorus of Def Leppard's *Pour Some Sugar On Me*.

# 16

## LUCIFER

We may have entered from the side entrance but there is more than enough people around to see the commotion Lily is causing.

"Yes, dear, a strip club. I have a business meeting here tonight and it's our newest purchase. I want to see the changes that have been made."

She growls out to me through gritted teeth. "I thought you were taking me somewhere special!"

"I am."

Simon comes up from behind me and he nudges my shoulder. "They sent Marco Romano and his two associates."

Turning my gaze away from Lilith to the three men sitting in the middle of the club, I resist the urge to grin.

They sent a high-level shot caller to meet with me. He's not exactly the top tier in their organization, but he's there to show that they want to hear what I have to offer. This guy will be able to make a snap decision or call someone who can right away.

Snapping my fingers at Simon, I say, "Ensure they have anything they want before I get to the table. Anything they want is to come from the top shelf."

"Got it."

Pulling Lilith to the side of the entrance, I look down into her eyes. Those fucking emerald chips are staring daggers at me.

"The men we are about to sit with are here for a very serious matter. It doesn't matter where the fuck the location is. Do not embarrass me, this is our life, Lilith."

I look around the club, then pushing us further into the corner I grab her chin so that I can hold her eyes.

She wants to say something but I don't give her the chance. Leaning down I kiss her lips hard. Pushing my tongue into her mouth, I feel her instant reaction to fight me, but I don't give up.

Moments go by as she tries to resist me, but in the end, her hands are clutching at my shirt. Her breath comes out in hitches as I pull back.

My cock is ready to go right this moment but I will it down.

"We can't keep our guests waiting."

Tugging her hand lightly, I lead us into the club proper. The lights are low and the music is pumping through the speakers. As the last song fades away, White Zombie's *More Human Than Human* comes on.

Approaching the table, a tall buxom redhead stands in my way. Tall, with breasts as fake as her cherry red hair. She's the most popular stripper in every club she works. "Cherry Bomb, thanks for taking over the new venture."

She stalks up to me and I can't help but smile. This vixen is the absolute definition of sin.

"Lucifer, my only love..." She purrs as she literally wraps her body around me. She is not one for family hugs, no she makes sure her pussy mound is press firmly against me. "Where have you been? I miss you."

Pulling my hand from Lilith's, I untangle myself from Cherry and push her to a more comfortable distance from me. I have a personal bubble that should never be breached. She doesn't give one shit. If I let her, she would be weaving between my legs like a cat marking her territory.

Grabbing Lilith's hand, I pull her forward to stand beside me. "How are the new girls and the old girls working out?"

Standing up straight, Cherry switches from sex kitten to instant business mode. She is a certified CPA business school graduate, but this is, as she says, a much more interesting line of work. "Good. I've fired two of the old staff today during the mandatory meeting. They showed up late."

Nodding my head, I ask, "How's the bartender?"

"He's skimming two dollars for every ten."

"Have the police here at the end of the night. Make sure the new cameras catch him in the act."

"Will do. Anything else?" she asks.

"How are you enjoying managing the new club?"

"It's going to be one of the top earners."

Grinning, I nod. "Make sure it is."

Looking to Lilith, her face is inscrutable to me as she stares from Cherry to me and then back. "This is Lilith, be a good kitten and fetch us drinks, Cherry."

Just as quick as she went into business mode, Cherry's whole demeanor switches back to the sexual devil act. She nods as she brushes up against me, her cheek rubbing against my shoulder then she all but rubs herself against Lilith who just stands there, opened mouthed.

Poor girl has never met the likes of Cherry, I bet.

Walking us to the table where Marco sits, I smile to him

as he tears his eyes from the pale girl on the main stage. The dancer on stage is swirling around the pole, her head tilted way back as her pink dreads fly behind her.

Nodding to the girl, I grin at Romano.

He stands up from the table and his retinue is quick to follow. "Lucifer! Man is it good to see you have taken this place over. I wish we could have snapped it up ourselves!"

I reach out to shake his hand. "It was one of those perfect timing things, Marco. It's good seeing you again. Let me introduce Lilith."

Looking from me, to where Lilith and I hold hands, he offers her a warm smile. "It's good to meet you, Lilith."

Bowing his head low to her for a moment, Marco looks up and introduces his two me. "This is Anthony and Gio."

Shaking hands with everyone, we sit down as Simon comes up and grudgingly sits down with us.

Raising my glass, I say, "To new ventures!"

"New ventures!" Marco grins at me.

Yeah, the fucker knows I am looking to work with him.

Settling down in our chairs, Marco leans forward as he frowns at me. "Lucifer, let me first say before anything else is said, what happened in Ohio has my family very upset, but we don't have ties to anything that happened to you or your money. We know this could hurt our relationship with you, but…"

He lifts his shoulders in a 'what can I do' gesture.

It figures they would feel that way, and truthfully, they have no dog in the fight. Nodding my head, I say, "I know Marco, but I had to make sure I had the story before I made any judgments."

Nodding his head, he says, "It's a clusterfuck up there right now. There is an interim head for now… But we will see what happens. The fucking Irish, though, are bringing in some fucking crazy bastard from Ireland in to make things settle down… it's going to be interesting, to say the least."

That's news on both fronts of what's happening in the Midwest region. I don't know whether he is intentionally dropping information for me or it's an accident but it's giving me an inside look.

"Now that that's been said, let me ask? How the fuck do I fall into such a good joint like this?"

Laughing, I smile at him. "Next time I find a club that looks like a good buy I'll call you, let you have first dibs. Sound good?"

"Deal."

Smiling, I say, "So let's talk about you and the Yakuza."

Frowning, he says, "The scum sucking bastards. They have been pushing further and further into our streets. Each day we see their little fucking wrappers they have their heroin wrapped in littering the fucking streets, trash everywhere. Half the time their shit isn't cut right and it's killing people off."

I can feel his annoyance. I haven't seen much but I have seen enough of them to know they are starting to feel like they can sell on other people's turf.

"How much of the docks have they tried to take over so far?" I ask.

Lifting his eyebrows at me in surprise, he frowns at me. "I didn't know that was common news yet."

"It's not, Marco. Don't worry about that. I am just very well informed when it comes to Garden City."

"They haven't got much but they are trying pretty damn hard to buy out all the contracts there."

"Do you guys need help with that? I know a few men down there."

He pulls back from me as he looks at my face, trying to

gauge my intent. I have just put my side next to his without asking for anything. Right now, I bet he is wondering why.

"Well... Lucifer, I have to be honest. That would go a long way with my people and yours forming a good partnership."

He's right, it would help them. The only reason I have yet to claim the docks is because of the headache it would be taking something that's so near the Russians. The Italians would be best for both factions if they took it.

But it could just as easily be the Yakuza.

I could have offered the same position to the Yakuza, but when someone spits in my face I don't tend to feel generous.

"You know I am going to ask why us and not the Japs," he states after he takes a long drink from his scotch.

"You didn't put up airs when I asked for a meeting. You know I am a valuable person to work with."

"Fair enough. If you would put the call in we would be very appreciative," he says, nodding his head as he puts emphasis on *appreciative*.

"Good, it's settled. I'll make the call tonight." I snap my fingers at Cherry Bomb who has been waiting off to one side.

Leaning to me, Cherry puts her ear next to my lips. I take in a breath of her skin as I say, "Have the pink dreaded girl and any others who catch the guys fancy taken to the private rooms."

"Yes, sir," she purrs back to me then walks towards the back and motions to a few of the girls.

Cherry has a certain smell about her, it's a mixture of some heady pheromone she exudes as a perfume. That smell use to affect me in ways I didn't allow myself to act on. Now? It smells like something annoying.

Lilith's scent alone causes me to feel primordial and possessive. It pulls me to her, keeping my very being locked on her. Whether she understands it or not, Lilith is mine and just the thought of another woman doing nothing for me is enough for me to know I am hooked on her forever.

Looking back to Marco, I say, "If you guys need anything tonight let Cherry know, she will make sure you have it."

Grinning to me, he nods but then looks like he has come to a decision. "Because we didn't want to seem like you owed us anything, I have information on the Yakuza and the man they are using, Marshall."

Instantly my interest is peaked. "You said they are *using*?"

"Yeah, it looks like he has gone to them for something. We don't know what but he's been there for an hour. We just found out right before we got here. My uppers wanted to make sure you knew."

Nodding my head, I say, "Thank you, Marco, it's very appreciated."

Smiling, he nods. "My appreciation is much returned, friend."

Nodding to us both, he says, "And Lilith, forgive me for not asking… You are?"

"She's my wife," I say as I turn to smile at Lilith.

"Congratulations Lucifer!" he says, lifting his glass to us both.

Looking to Lilith, there's a stunned expression on her face, and out of the corner of my eyes I can see Simon shaking his head slightly.

Lilith turns to speak to me but with a shake of my head she clamps her mouth shut. Now is not the time for us to have this conversation. I think she can tell that when I grip her hand in my own.

Cherry comes to the table with a group of girls and they start pulling the Italians up from their chairs. Smiling, the Italians wave goodbye to us as they get ushered to the back of the building. Cherry follows them all, my insurance that things will go as expected.

Turning to Simon, I snap, "Find out what the fuck Marshall is doing with the fucking Yakuza. *Now*."

At first he is taken aback by the information then he nods. "On it."

We should have had that damn information.

He leans down to my ear as he is getting ready to leave. "Do I need to get the paperwork and filings dealt with?"

Nodding my head, I say to him, "Yes."

"Need a ring?"

Frowning at him, I tell him, "I can do that on my own."

Nodding his head, he shoots out of the club. I am mystified on how the fuck he didn't have that information but I am sure he will get it soon.

He better, because right now we look like idiots.

## 17

LILY

*I* can't believe I'm sitting here, listening in on some kind of mob deal going down. How did my life get to this? Is this my fault? Is this the consequence of all my bad decisions?

The fact that Marshall's name is brought up doesn't surprise me in the least. Now I know what he's been up to all these years. It wasn't just his mistresses in every city, these kind of under the table deals are how he made his money.

I've been so oblivious, so damn willfully blind, I know deep down inside I have no one to blame but myself for this.

Tonight started off on such a high note, but now I feel deflated, like someone let all the air out of me.

I feel like an absolute idiot for thinking Lucifer was taking me out on a date. I spent all day getting ready for a nice night out, some time away from the children. Just me and him, getting to know each other…

And he brings me to a freaking strip club.

I was so angry at him when we walked in I could of spit, but worst of all I was angry at myself. Of course he would bring me to a strip club. That's the kind of man he is, and I shouldn't have let myself forget it.

What did I think, that we were dating or something? It's just sex. I'm just his *possession*.

Gah, I probably deserve this, especially since I didn't turn on my heel and walk out right away. And especially when I didn't smack that slutty redhead.

Lucifer stopped me from walking out, but to be honest I let him stop me. It wasn't his kisses that subdued me but the words he let slip. He did it deliberately, I know it now, but still my curiosity got the best of me.

He made it sound like I have a stake in all of this.

He called this club *our* business, said this is *our* life, and those guests waiting at the table we're *our* guests, like I have something to lose or gain out of all of this.

Do I own part of this club, is that what he's suggesting? Am I a part of this business deal that's about to go down?

*Probably not*, I sigh and sink down in my seat. Tipping my drink back, I peer up at him through my lashes while he and the men we're sitting across from talk about things I don't understand.

Lucifer has a way with words, a way with people, and I'm just one of many in a long string of his victims.

Watching him, I'm starting to get it. It's not just his stunning looks that draw people in, it's the way he carries himself, the way he talks. The way he moves his hands. Manipulation just comes naturally to him.

I'm not even sure he's aware he's doing it, but he probably is. Who needs a gun or a knife when your words are a weapon?

But it's not just the words, is it? It's *how* he speaks them.

Lifting my drink to my lips, I turn my eyes to the dark-haired man he is currently engaged in conversation with. It's not just the women that are weak to Lucifer—seriously, just about every pair of female eyes in the club tonight keep sneaking peeks in our direction—it's also these men.

The men were stiff when we approached, the smiles on their lips there out of pretense, but now the smiles are very real and they're very relaxed.

And all after a few words with Lucifer. It's like everyone is best of friends.

He talks to them so easily, and the way he talks too just makes you want to listen. To give him your full attention.

I'm too busy, though, keeping track of my nemesis—the red-headed stripper that greeted us when we first walked in.

*Why do I even care?* I keep asking myself. I'm having all these sudden revelations about Lucifer and the kind of man he is yet that woman is making me feel insanely jealous.

It doesn't make any damn sense.

I don't like the way she looks at him, and I definitely don't like the way she keeps finding a way to touch him.

I swear to God he *smelled* her when she dropped our drinks off and I just about stood up and scratched her eyes out right then and there.

Reminding myself that I don't like Lucifer, he's not mine, and she can have him if she wants him, was the only thing that brought me back to my senses.

Seriously, I don't want him. He's up for grabs…

Yet, something about *her* wanting him makes me want him.

It's driving me to distraction.

Vaguely, I'm aware that business is being wrapped up. My attention though is on Cherry, the red-head, as she saunters over with a sly glint in her eyes and a smirk curling at the corners of her lips.

"She's my wife," Lucifer says and looks at me.

My blood goes cold and all the color drains from my face. Who is?

"Congratulations, Lucifer!" the dark-haired man lifts his glass towards us.

Us? As in me?

Did I get married and not remember it? Wouldn't I have to get divorced first? I know I'm not a widow, Marshall is still kicking and breathing. They were just talking about him…

Lucifer smiles at me and gives me that look he likes to give. The one that he gave me earlier when he warned me not to fuck this up for him or there will be dire consequences.

Why did he just lie to them about us being married? What purpose does that serve? Is this just another way to keep me trapped with him?

I throw the rest of my drink back, I'm so done with this shit.

Cherry and a bunch of other girls pull the guys up from their seats and lead them into the back. Simon approaches and bends over Lucifer's ear. He and Lucifer have a super-secret whisper conversation.

Glass empty, I set it down on the table and stand from my chair.

I walk around the table and Lucifer's hand snatches out, grabbing my hand.

"Where are you going?" he asks, his eyes full of suspicion as he tugs me closer to him.

"I need to use the ladies room," I snap. "I'm sorry, should I have asked your permission?"

He stares hard at me, his icy eyes bright and piercing. Spine stiffening, I hold his gaze and give as good as I get.

With a sigh, his grip loosens and he nods his head as if

giving me permission. "The ladies room is next to the bar. Do you want me to go with you?"

"No," I grit between my teeth and yank my hand back.

Chin lifting into the air, I head towards the bar and hear Lucifer snapping his fingers behind my back. A moment later, James peels away from the shadows and follows behind me.

"For shit's sake, am I not even allowed to use the restroom by myself?" I mutter.

James chuckles and I shoot an angry glare over my shoulder. He's lucky I don't have a glass to throw at his head.

"Wait here," he tells me when we reach the bathroom and uses his thick arm as a bar to block me from walking in.

"Is this really necessary?" I ask.

He doesn't even look at me as he answers, "Yes."

Damn. If there's a worry that I could be taken out in the ladies' room, my life has seriously gone in the wrong direction.

With a huff, I take a step back, cross my arms over my chest and wait for him to finish his inspection.

"You've got five minutes," he tells me when he's finished. He plants himself in front of the swinging door, blocking anyone else from coming in.

"Make it ten," I call out as I hustle in. "I need to touch up my makeup."

"Eight, and you're pushing it."

I flip him the bird and hear him mutter, "Little hellcat," under his breath.

I take care of my business in under a minute, wash my hands and check my makeup. With fives minute to spare, I walk over to the lone window in the room and try to shove it open.

It doesn't give.

Shit.

Head tipping back, I peek up at the ceiling. It's completely solid. There has to be a way out of this place...

"You can't go in," I hear James tell somebody.

"It's just me, you know I won't try anything," I hear Cherry purr.

"It's not up to me, take it up with the boss."

"Okay, I'll go get him..."

"You do that."

I hear Cherry snort and then her heels are tapping away.

Shaking my head, I put her out of my mind and check the other stalls for an escape option.

"Two minutes!" James calls out.

"I'm almost done," I call back.

I swear, this crap makes me feel like a little kid.

There are no other ways out, only the window. Walking back up to it, I push and shove with all my might but it won't budge. I check the seal; it's been nailed shut.

Dammit.

I don't even know what I would do if I could get it open, I just want to get out of here. I feel the need to at least try to get myself out of this mess, even if it's hopeless.

He has my kids locked up in his compound. Even if I did manage to somehow to get away, there's no way I could leave without them.

"Everything alright?" James asks, his head popping in.

Leaning against the sink, I wipe at my eyes and nod my head.

"Shit," James curses and takes a step back out, looking very uncomfortable. "I'm sorry. Take as long as you like..."

Shaking my head, I push away from the sink. Tearing off a paper towel, I use it to dab at the corners of my eyes and blow my nose. "I'm sorry, I just needed a minute but I'm ready now. Do I look okay?"

James swallows and looks me up and down. "You look beautiful," he says gruffly and turns away.

"Thanks," I say to his back and follow him out into the club.

The first thing I see as we walk back into the main room is Cherry leaning over Lucifer's chair, the two of them laughing and talking. Her fake breasts are all up in his face and her ass is sticking up in the air, inches away from his hand. She's freaking shameless, but he doesn't seem to be bothered by her behavior.

The way he's looking at her, the way he lets her get so familiar with him is like a knife to my heart. My feet just stop. I can't keep walking.

James notices immediately and turns towards me with a worried look.

Tearing my gaze away from the two lovebirds, I plead to James. "Take me home, please."

James casts his worried look towards Lucifer then back to me. "I'm sorry, I can't do that…"

Finally, Lucifer looks up from Cherry, noticing me. Cherry casts a little glance over her shoulder and then straightens away from him.

More words are exchanged between them. James shifts uncomfortably. I know I'm putting him in a bad position. With a nod and a smirk on her lips, Cherry saunters away from Lucifer, wiggling her ass as she heads for the back.

Looking towards me, Lucifer motions for me to approach him.

"Come on," James says more firmly. "You don't want to make a scene. You know it won't end well if you do."

I cast one last, hopeless glance around the club. He's right. I don't have any friends here. What choice do I have?

I concentrate on putting one foot in front of the other. It helps a little that the stage lights up and the music starts pumping. Reaching Lucifer's table, I try to walk back to my chair but he grabs me by the hand and yanks me down to his lap.

"Everything all right?" he asks.

I turn my eyes to the stage, avoiding the question.

"Lilith," Lucifer growls and grabs me by the chin. He turns my face back, forcing me to look at him.

His eyes search my face. "What's wrong? Did something happen?"

What's wrong? Is he serious? There's so much wrong with this, all of this, I can't even begin to explain it.

Willing my bottom lip not to tremble, I say softly, carefully, "I want to go home."

"We can't leave yet. We've got at least a couple more hours before Marco and his men are done in the back."

I shake my head and then take a deep, steadying breath. "I want to go to *my* home. I can't do this. Please."

"What the fuck happened?" he asks more forcefully, his grip tightening.

My eyes blur with tears but I blink them away. I will not cry, dammit. "Nothing happened. I just want to go."

He shakes his head but his grip loosens. "We've already had this discussion, Lilith."

"Why?" I ask, almost choking on my desperation.

"Why, what?" he repeats, reaching around me to pick up his glass.

I hate this, and I hate him. Can't he see that? Being kept in his house, disconnected from everything in that safe little bubble he created, made it so much easier to accept. But being out here, in the real world, makes me aware again of how sick it is.

"Why do you want to keep me? You have an entire club full of women that want you."

And I'm sure that there are many more out there that

want him.

He takes a deep drink from his glass, his eyes assessing me above the rim before he asks, "Don't you want me, Lily?"

"No," is my knee-jerk response.

He tips his head back and laughs. "Liar."

Setting my jaw, I turn my face away to look at the stage again. Needing a break from this madness.

"Lily," he purrs and his fingers are gentle this time as they turn my head back to him. "I want you. I don't want them."

"Why?" I ask, feeling a rogue tear slip down my cheek.

"Because you're beautiful."

I snort softly at that and his grip tightens. "Because you're fucking sexy."

"This entire room is full of beautiful, half-naked women that are sexier than me," I argue weakly.

He leans close to me, his lips a hair away from kissing me. "Because you're mine. You were made for me."

I open my mouth to argue with him and he presses his advantage. His lips crush against my lips as his hand grips me, keeping me from escaping the kiss.

By the time he pulls away, I'm struggling to catch my breath. His grip around my jaw loosens and his thumb strokes along my bottom lip.

"You drive me fucking crazy," he growls. "Can't you feel what you're doing to me?"

My brain is so fuzzy from the kiss it takes me a moment to remember what I wanted to say. Beneath me, I can feel him growing hard and poking me uncomfortably. Regardless of how angry with him I am, I can feel my body responding.

My core tightening.

"Any woman here would probably be thrilled to be yours," I argue and try to pull away. "Why keep me? Why force me? Just go have your way with Cherry."

Lucifer scowls at me and shakes his head. "I should have known bringing you here would bring out your insecurities."

"My what?" I sputter at him as he leans back and lifts his glass to his lips. Tipping his head back, he drains the rest of his drink.

"I'm not insecure," I go on. "I could care less. I just want you to let me go..."

Glass empty, Lucifer lowers it and his eyes flash with mischief as he grins at me. I hate that grin. If I was braver I'd smack it off his face.

"It's alright, kitten. I know what you need."

Leaning forward, he rests his empty glass on the table and then grabs me by the hips, lifting me. Planting me on my feet, he grabs my hand, stopping me before I can walk away. Rising from the chair behind me, he straightens to his full height.

18

LILY

Tugging me by the hand, Lucifer leads me forward, towards the back of the club, and my heart pounds wildly.

What does he mean to do to me? What does he think I need?

I should have just kept my big mouth shut. Tonight, my stupid is really showing.

We pass through an open doorway and the light dims, the music softens. He leads me down a long, red-carpeted hallway.

There are a few open doorways, the only door being at the end. A bouncer is standing up against the wall ahead of us. His beefy arms are crossed in front of his chest and he has a bored expression on his face.

I can hear moans, giggles, and the sound of flesh slapping.

The bouncer glances towards us and nods at Lucifer. "Evening, boss."

Lucifer smiles easily and comes to a stop, pausing in front of the doorway. "Good evening, Bruce. How's it going?"

The three of us turn our attention to the open room. I get an eyeful of a saggy ass thrusting into a moaning Cherry and immediately turn away.

Fuck, I really wish I didn't just see that.

Bruce shrugs his shoulders. "It's going."

Lucifer chuckles and gives him a slap on the shoulder. "Alright. I'll be in my office. Don't let anyone disturb me unless it's an emergency."

Bruce nods and Lucifer is tugging me forward once more. I'm so anxious to get away from the scene I just glimpsed I almost run ahead of him.

Pushing the door at the end of the hallway open, Lucifer pushes me inside. Stumbling ahead, I nearly fall on my face as he slams the door behind me.

The loud click of the lock registers in my brain. I'd take in the room but it's so dark I can't see.

"Lucifer?" I ask, my voice trembling. He isn't locking me in here, is he?

"Don't worry, I'm right here, Lily," he says from behind me.

There's a pause and then the light flickers on.

Lucifer is standing in front of the door, his eyes bright as he stares at me.

I take a step back and look at my surroundings. There's no window, no other doors or means of escape. Just a large mahogany desk, a few chairs, and a filing cabinet.

Shedding his coat and hanging it up on the rack beside him, he tells me to, "Remove your dress."

I take a step back. "Why?"

Loosening the tie at his neck, he grins wickedly. "Because I told you to."

He takes a step forward and I take another step back. I

know there's no possible way for me to escape but the way he's looking at me, the pure hunger that's openly displayed on his face, is frightening me.

I can't tell if he wants to kill me or fuck me.

Or both.

"Because the sight of the other women has done nothing for me but left me wanting you…"

I shake my head and back myself up against his desk.

"Because we didn't get to finish what we started in the car."

He yanks his tie out of his collar and grips it in his fist as he strides forward, eating up the distance I created. "Because I can only spend so much time in your presence without fucking you before I start going mad with lust."

Walking into me, he looms over me as I bend back. "Because I fucking told you to, Lily. Obey or face the fucking consequences."

Tears sting my eyes as I struggle to reach behind myself and pull down the zipper that runs the length of my back. "Why are you doing this?" I ask.

Grabbing me, impatient, he spins me around and then shoves me forward until I'm bent over, my hands hitting his desk. "Because you need it."

Yanking my zipper down, I feel the fabric of my dress spread and the cool air chills my skin. "Are you done with the fucking questions?"

He pulls my sleeves down my shoulders. "Well?" he snaps when I don't answer him. Lifting each of my hands, he keeps me bent over as he slides my dress down my chest then over my hips and finally down my legs.

"Yes," I answer, stiffening as he bends over me again.

His hardness brushes against my ass and I flinch away from him.

Grabbing me by the hips, he pulls me back, grinding me

against his erection. "Feel what you do to me, Lily. You make me fucking weak."

My eyes nearly roll into the back of my head and a pulsing throb awakens between my thighs.

I could argue that I'm the one that's weak to him, unable to resist him no matter how angry I am. This blade cuts both ways, and we're both victims to this thing between us.

He touches me and my body comes alive beneath his hands. Just the faint touch of his breath against my skin is enough to get my blood boiling. I'm starting to forget what life was like, what it felt like to exist before him.

For so long I was dead inside and when he touches me I'm resurrected.

His hands roam up, covering and squeezing my breasts. His breath is hot against my throat and I arch my neck as he growls. "You're like a fucking drug. Your smell, your touch, your taste. I'm addicted. No other woman will do for me."

Just the thought of him being with another woman, of remembering him laugh and be so easy with Cherry, causes my little green-eyed monster to rear its ugly head.

He's broken me in ways I never thought I'd be broken. I shouldn't crave his attention; I shouldn't crave his affection. Yet I want it, I need it.

He's infecting me with his sickness.

Reaching around my back, one hand unsnaps my bra while the other grabs my breast as it spills free. "I should hate you for what you've done to me. For the way you've trapped me. But I have this inexplicable need to protect you, to take care of you."

His fingers stroke down my back and I bite my lip to muffle my cry as they slide into my panties. "You've become precious to me."

His nails scratch down my mons and through what little

hair down there I keep trimmed. "You can keep fighting me, Lily, but I'll just keep fucking you until you love me."

*I will never love you*, I think. He can take my body, he can elicit compliance from me, but he can't force his way into my heart. I'll harden it against this illness.

No matter how good this feels, no matter how much I fucking *need* him, I can't let myself love him. It's the one thing I have left that he can't wrestle from me. My last bastion of resistance.

Falling in love with him would be like falling in love with death.

"Fucking hell, you're already so wet for me," he growls appreciatively as his fingers slide through me. "If I had the patience I'd eat your sweet little pussy."

Grabbing me by the hips, he spins me around. I gasp as my world tilts and I lose my balance.

Steadying me, he looms over me, his face dark and full of menace. Straps sliding down my arms, he removes my bra and pushes me down.

As he bends me back, spreading me out on his desk, he lifts my hands above my head. The tie he removed from his neck is wound around my wrists and knotted.

Reaching down, he rips my panties down my legs and my stilettos fall off.

"Look at you," he purrs, stepping back to admire me.

I curl my fingers and test the tightness of my restraint. It doesn't give.

Panting heavily, I'm on the verge of hyperventilating, the edges of my vision wavering as he unsnaps his pants.

"Stay like that, just like that, Lily," he purrs. "If you move, you'll walk out of here without your dress."

Stiff as a board, I lay on the hard, unforgiving desk. My heart pounding behind my ribs and my breasts rising and falling with my pants.

I watch him take his cock in his hand and feel a twinge deep inside as he pumps his fist slowly up and down his shaft.

His eyes scorch over my body, drinking me in. Stepping forward, I almost move. I almost open my legs wider for him.

"Such a good little kitten," he purrs and his lips smirk down at me as the crown his cock bumps against my entrance.

A flash of anger rises up in me and I narrow my eyes up at him.

He laughs.

Bending down, his fingers slip around my neck. Lifting my head off the desk, he says, "Did I ever tell you how beautiful you are when you're angry?"

His lips smash against my lips as his cock thrusts inside me, spearing me mercilessly on his long shaft.

I'm already so wet, so swollen, there's no resistance. All my little muscles relax around him, hugging him tight then gripping him. Pulling him in.

Groaning into my mouth, he rears back then slams himself deep again. He's so big, so thick, I'm experiencing that raw feeling of satisfaction again.

Fucking hell, I needed this. I needed him inside me. I needed this connection.

I needed to be conquered by him.

"Feeling better already?" he asks as I relax beneath him.

Pushing up, his eyes lock on my eyes and I try to look away. He grabs my face and forces me to look at him.

With his gaze alone he's stripping me of my layers, of all my little protections. He's peering into the very depths of my soul as his hips roll against me in a deep, grinding rhythm.

My clit pulses, trapped. The pressure that was slowly building inside me swells and increases.

A low moan escaping my lips, he grins and begins to slam his cock into me harder. Faster.

Arching beneath him, my muscles tense up and my nails dig into the palms of my hands.

"Don't ever ask to leave me again," he snarls and slams into me so hard the desk creaks beneath us.

"The next time you ask I'll chain you to our fucking bed."

The pressure inside me just keeps building and building, threatening to burst from my skin.

"You belong with me. Your fucking home is wherever I am."

The throbbing, the aching is so overwhelming as he pounds himself into me, I'm not sure how much more I can stand.

"I'll never let you go. Never. They'll have to pry you from my cold, dead hands," he roars out and pounds into me as my body locks up, fighting through the tight clench of my sex.

All at once my climax hits me. The pressure that was building deep in my belly exploding in a white flash.

Warmth fills me, Lucifer grunts and growls above me. For one glorious moment we're on the same plane, coexisting in this orgasmic madness.

Wave after wave of pleasure pulses through my limbs. I'm twitching, arching and straining against my bonds—his weight above me and the tie around my wrists.

He settles first, coming down on top of me with a sigh, spent.

While I'm still convulsing and twitching beneath him.

He holds me, stroking me through the last of my spasms until I go still, all the strength draining from my limbs.

When the last flutter settles and he's sliding out of me, I open my eyes to find him staring down at me with an unreadable expression as he does up his pants.

Reaching above me, he pulls my arms down and silently

unbinds my hands. Lifting my wrists to his lips, he kisses all the spots where the tie dug into my skin.

Straightening to his full height, he offers me a hand up then helps me step into my dress. Pushing my hands gently away, he pulls my dress up and then zips the zipper up my back. He treats me with such care, with such tenderness, I don't know what to make of it.

I'm left reeling after everything that just happened.

My hair a wild, unruly mess, he extracts what's left of my pins and then brushes it out with his fingers. I just stare at him in confusion. How can he be so intense and demanding one moment and so sweet the next?

Brushing my curls over my shoulders, he finally breaks the silence.

His voice raw and thick, he says, "Now you know what you mean to me. In the future, I trust you won't forget it."

19

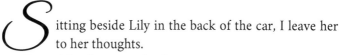

LUCIFER

Sitting beside Lily in the back of the car, I leave her to her thoughts.

She isn't broken completely, yet.

She's like a wild horse in some ways, just biding her time until she is able to get to freedom. She doesn't understand, though, that she is too accustomed to the straps I have wrapped around her heart and mind. She needs that ray of hope that she will be free of me someday soon because to her I am the monster she must rebel against.

This isn't right to her, this isn't real for her. Silly girl.

Lily wants my collar, she needs it.

All of her life she has searched for something to fill that void left deep inside of her. She needs someone to take her as his, to give her meaning and definition, even if she doesn't understand that herself.

Turning from the window, Lily looks at me as I stare at the curves and angles of her beautiful face. Her eyes are dark and full of uncertainty. "Why does everyone call you Lucifer?"

Shrugging my shoulders, I say, "I got the name when I was a teenager. It stuck."

"What's the story behind it, though? Why? The name surely is… crass and makes people afraid of you."

"That's why it sticks so well. I want them afraid."

"So, man of mystery, how did you get the name?" she asks with a smirk.

"My stepsister first called me it when I was fourteen."

"You have a sister?" she asks, looking almost confused.

"Yeah. Why do you seem shocked?"

"I just kind of figured you…Well, you would have eaten any competition."

Laughing out loud, I smile at her. She has the rights to it, though. If my stepsister and I had been closer in age, I would have.

I reach across the seat to the buckle she has strapped across her chest. Pushing the button, I let it slide across her stomach. Reaching over, I pull her to my chest as I lean back against the door.

"You're probably right about that. I would have if she wasn't five years older than me. She was very fond of teasing me about being so serious about becoming my father's heir."

"You're saying *was*."

"She's not dead if that's what you're wondering, just on another continent. After I took over I gave her enough money to live comfortably. She is and was a pain in the ass to deal with. Anyways, one day a man had scaled the wall of the villa we lived in. He wanted to break into the place since he thought nobody would be home, steal our things then leave. I caught him in the act."

"What did you do?"

"I tortured him. I made him give up his entire life, from

the first theft he ever committed to where his mother and sister lived."

"Why? I mean, sure he was an idiot but why not call the police?"

"Because I wanted a message sent. I wanted the world to know if they wouldn't fuck with my father, then they dare not fuck with me."

My fingers are twined into Lily's hands as I feel her stiffen up. She wanted to know though. She needs to know the man she belongs to, needs to understand that this is his life and by extension hers—though she will never need to fear anything but my wrath.

I will pull the reaper by the fucking throat if he ever dares fuck with her.

"The screams couldn't be contained fully so by the time I finished him Meredith was there to cast judgment on me. She didn't know what he had planned to do to our home or us, she only saw that I had hurt a man. Hurt a man who was begging for the life of his mother."

Pulling away from, me she sits up fully. "So, she saw the devil, right?"

"Yeah, she actually called me that. She said, 'You're the fucking devil! You're Lucifer.' And it stuck. The guards first started calling me it, not unkindly. They saw that I was cut from the same cloth as my father, maybe more. Father took notice of it, especially after he learned of what I had done. I think he called me it out of some pride, maybe terror as well. He knew I was far more ruthless than he could ever be."

Shuddering slightly, she allows me to pull her back to my chest. "You see, Lily, I was protecting my sister and myself. There is nothing in this world I won't do to protect those I love and call my own. Nothing. You, Adam and Evie are mine. I will protect you all until the end of time."

PULLING up in front of the house, I step out of the car with Lily. Taking my coat off of myself, I wrap it around her. She may have a coat on but the wind has picked up in intensity. The freezing bite is hitting our skin even harder than when we left.

Wind whipping my suit jacket around me, I pull her to me as we reach the doors. Pulling her tight to my body, I press my mouth hard against her own as I push her up against the front door. My tongue dives into her mouth as I feel her wrap a leg tightly around me, her mound pushing hard against me.

Forcing myself away from her is like poisoning myself. Each moment away I feel the pain of being separated. I may own her, but she has claimed a part of me just as well.

"Goodnight Lily, I'll be back late tonight. I have business to deal with before I can come to bed."

"But…" she starts to protest. Shaking my head, I open the door and assist her in.

Stepping back out into the winter storm that has been brewing for the last few hours, I smile at her then turn back to the car. Getting into the warmth of the car, I shake off any of the humanity I showed to Lily.

"Andrew, take us towards the office."

"Yes, sir."

Pulling out my cell phone, I dial Simon. "What do we know?"

"I was getting ready to call you just now. Can you get to Marshall's house? I have something I need to show you."

"Do you want to talk about it?" I ask him after I give Andrew our destination.

"No, I don't think I do. You need to see this for yourself. We definitely have an issue."

Swiping off the phone, I growl. Whatever happened at Marshall's has Simon staying quiet which is never a good sign. More than likely he is keeping silent because he doesn't want anything we have to say possibly being overheard with any kind of detection.

Fuck me, tonight's going to be a long night.

~

Pulling up beside Simon's car, he motions for me to follow. We're not too close to Marshall's house, about half a block down the street from him, but it's not hard to see what has Simon's attention as he leads me down to Thomas' personal car. It's a black, late model, BMW that he bought after the last one was totaled chasing down a guy who owed us a fuck ton of money.

Coming up to the side of the car, I see that the driver side window is shattered completely, destroyed by a bullet. The entrance wound is on the side of his head. The exit wound has left the right side of his face missing. This isn't a small caliber type of bullet wound. From the large hole in the right-side car door, I can only assume someone decided to make sure he was dead.

Looking across the field I see a couple of spots that could hide a sniper.

Walking up to my side, Simon points to the rocks building into a hill. "Large caliber, off that hill over there."

"Any evidence left?" I ask.

"Just a shell and a couple of cigarette butts. Looks like they are from a Japanese cigarette manufacturing company."

Nodding my head, I say, "This explains how we didn't see Marshall disappearing only to end up with the Yakuza."

"Yeah, I am guessing so. But something feels wrong about

it. I mean, why the fuck would they even care about Marshall or feel the need to kill Thomas?

"We need more information," I say as I stand up from looking at the mess.

Sighing, I walk back to my car with Simon by my side. "Get a guy over to Thomas' mother's house. Let her know what's going on and see that she and his sister will be taken care of financially, indefinitely."

"Got it. I need to make a call, I want to see if they really do have him in their hands. And I need to check to with a guy I know inside of their group who may know about what they are up to."

"Go for it, but bring me two of their men if Marshall is indeed in their hands. I don't give a fuck who they are or what they could know, just bring me two of them. Meet me at the warehouse."

"You sure..." Simon starts to say.

Looking at him, I don't bother to reply. This is my fucking outfit, he will do as I fucking want.

Getting into the car, I nod to Andrew as I say, "Pay your last respects, Andrew, to Thomas. Make sure you understand what they did to him."

Getting out of the car, Andrew walks up to the BMW. He stands there for a long moment before coming back to the car.

When he gets in I say to him, "Contact our good friend Detective Sommers. Let him know that there is an issue here he will be getting contacted about. We want him to fully investigate the situation."

"Yes, sir." There is a small hitch in his voice as he shifts the vehicle into drive.

"Let's head to the warehouse."

SIMON CALLS me on the way to the warehouse.

His voice stiff as he says, "My contact has dropped off of the face of the earth, and from what I'm hearing, Marshall was seen going into their little compound on his own free will."

"You trust the source saw him?"

"Yeah, completely, it's a video feed after all."

Smirking, I say, "Bring me two of their men."

"Got one, I'll have Thaddeus bring another."

"Good."

The snow bursts from the sky, eventually turning all the ugly fucking dirty gray world back into a white covered shit hole again.

Sitting outside of the warehouse, we wait for my men's arrival.

Already present, though, is James along with Peter. The men are all sitting in the car with me now. I tried to reassure them I am perfectly safe on my own but even they will not bother to listen to me. It seems the death of Thomas has them feeling protective and murderous.

Simon arrives first with Philip sitting beside a gagged man in the backseat of the car. The man is thrashing around in the seat.

Getting out of the SUV, I stand by as James and Philip yank the screaming man from the car. He's gagged but his screams reach a fevered pitch.

Little bitch knows he's in the shit, I guess.

I follow behind them as I talk to Simon. "What's with your contact's silence?"

"More than likely he was made in some way. Not surprised but I would have preferred he fucked up at another time."

"You and me both. Still, things will proceed regardless. Anything I should know?"

"I called around a bit on the way here. Looks like they are taking over the docks by force right now. Not much the Italians would have been able to do without us. Do you want me to send out the troops?"

"Yeah, I do. Take whatever space the Yakuza have there for the Italians. Then keep our guys there to act as guards. Keep all inner circle men on a two-man cycle. I want the buddy system in place as of right now. They are to be in pairs until this issue is resolved."

Rolling his eyes, he says, "That means me included, doesn't it?"

Chuckling, I nod my head. "Yeah, you and Philip. Me and Andrew, so on and so forth. From this point on, Paul will be with the children at all times. James as well. I want Bart on Lilith at all times when she is not in the home."

We enter into the back room as the men are securing down the man. His eyes are darting around wildly as he takes in all of us surrounding him.

Removing my jacket, I hand it to Andrew. Rolling up the sleeves of my white dress shirt, I walk over to the guy, "I doubt you have information that will be of value to us, but I'm going to check."

Ripping the tape and gag from the mouth of the guy, I look into his brown eyes. "You're going to die tonight. Do not doubt it, and it's going to be painful regardless of what you do or do not tell me. But I'll make you a deal. You tell me everything you know and I don't kill your whole fucking family."

A wad of spit lands on my eyebrow as he sneers, "They will know where I'm at, you pile of shit…"

Laughing loudly, a couple of the guys behind me start to chuckle. "Oh, I am positive they do, dead boy. They just won't be able to do shit about it."

His eyes widen as I slam my fist into his jaw. My knuckles

feel the tingling sensation as they connect with the man's jawbone.

"Now, why is Marshall coming to your group?" I ask calmly.

The next twenty minutes go much the same way except I have switched out with another man. I stand back, watching the interrogation go on. They say torture doesn't work on getting information out of people, but I find that to be a lie.

It works just fine for me tonight.

Bart is bringing in the second man as I walk over to the first, putting the pistol to his head. I say to him, "Your family is safe Haruto."

Pulling the trigger, I look into the eyes of the second man. His face is clean and unmarred by violence.

Shaking my head, I say, "Haruto had information for me. I hope you do too."

Walking over to the sink, I pick up a large bucket of water. Pointing to a second chair, I say, "Let's try this waterboarding thing. I hear it works wonders."

∽

THE LONG NIGHT has drained me of any humanity I may have had going into it.

Doing the things we did tonight always does that to a person. It's a hard life we lead, most would never be able to do the things we do. Those who can surround me.

The bodies have been dropped off at the homes of their families. I don't doubt the message I am sending will be received loud and clear.

A war has begun, now it's time for me to end it as swiftly as possible. I don't do the fight-here—fight-there type of fighting.

No, I drop the fucking bomb and walk away with a clear conscious.

Simon is in my car with me and he is dropped off first. "Simon, check on everything we got from those two. It wasn't much but the rumors of Marshall and a new pipeline of heroin is bothersome to me."

"I will. It might explain where he was for so long after the initial deal went south. Maybe he was with his source or with the Japanese."

I wait until we are at my own home to let my defenses down. The shoulder holster I have under my arm will be there for the time being until the uproar is done.

The day is just beginning as I walk in the door. I hear the running of feet as Evie comes tearing into the hall to greet me. She wraps her arms around my legs, "Heya! Missed you!"

She darts away again after a light hug and kiss on her cheek.

Adam comes in second to greet me. He is about to speak to me then stops as his eyes take in my whole person. Glancing at my reflection in the glass next to me, I can see what he sees. I have flecks of blood on me here and there. Looking down at my shirt, I see it's splattered as well. My gun is peeking out from under my armpit as I pull my suit jacket off.

"Sir... Evie has..." He stammers out before saying, "Sir... are you okay?"

I close my eyes for a moment then open them back up to look at him. "Yes, I'm fine, Adam, and do not call me sir. You may call me Matthew or Father if you wish, but not *sir*."

He gulps then says quietly, "Father are you sure? You have blood on you."

Squatting down before him, I nod. "It's not my own. It was another man's."

"What happened?"

"He was a part of a group who wanted to hurt our family so I stopped him."

"Good," he says quietly. "No one hurts us, right?"

Nodding my head, I stand up. "Was there something else you wanted to talk about?"

"Yes. I asked Evie what she wanted for her birthday and she told me it was a puppy. A real one but…"

"What's the problem?"

"Mommy has said we can't have one, they are too much work and…"

"I'll get your mother's approval. You just need to find a good breed that is very protective. I want you to research them before we go to pick one up."

Grinning from ear to ear he says, "Got it. Can I have one for my birthday too?"

"Would it drive your mother crazy?" I ask.

"Yes!"

"Then we already know the answer. But the same rules apply, it has to be very protective of you two. The animals must serve a useful purpose."

## 20

LILY

Sleeping without Lucifer in bed with me proved to be difficult last night.

The bed is much too big and much too cold without him in it. I spent most of the night tossing and turning, unable to rest without his arms around me. Without him pressed up against my back, keeping me trapped.

What was he doing out so late at night? Had he returned to the strip club? To Cherry? Or was he out hunting Marshall down?

I know Marshall was the topic of some unpleasant conversation last night and Lucifer seemed to be of a mind to do something about him.

Too many scenarios were running around in my brain for me to sleep comfortably.

Peeking at the clock, I see that it's a little after seven in the morning and Lucifer still isn't home yet.

Crawling out of bed, I shower and get dressed for the day,

and try not to worry about him. He's a big boy, he can take care of himself, obviously.

Still, I can't help but wonder where he is...

Checking the weather, it's bitterly cold outside which is completely normal for this time of the year, but it's the weekend. I'd like to take the kids out and do something. Maybe we could go see a movie together.

Checking myself one last time in the mirror, I pull open the bedroom door to see Lucifer approaching.

Immediately I feel my lips pulling into a smile and a pleasant warmth fills me. Is this happiness?

I hold the door open, my heart fluttering as I wait for him. His eyes sweep over me, warming with heat. Taking a step forward, I try to wrap my arms around him.

Shaking his head, he holds out his hand, pushing me away.

My heart falls instantly.

"Don't touch me right now, Lily."

My face falls and I jerk back. Why did he reject me? Did I do something wrong?

Before I can fully process the hurt, he grabs me by the arm and pulls me into the bedroom with him.

Shutting the bedroom door behind him, he grabs me by the arms and holds me away from him. "Let me get clean first. I don't want to get you bloody."

His words shock me into awareness.

Looking him over, I finally notice his shirt and pants are speckled with blood. "Are you hurt?"

He shakes his head and smiles at me tenderly. "It's not mine."

I return his smile for a moment. "That's good." As he relaxes and begins to pull away, I just have to ask, "Is it Marshall's?"

I wouldn't be surprised if he found him and did something to him.

He shakes his head and turns away. Loosening the tie at his throat, he yanks it out of his collar.

I don't know whether to be relieved or completely horrified that it wasn't Marshall but some other man splattering Lucifer with his blood last night.

Never in a million years did I ever think my life would come to something like this. That I'd ever have to accept these things as a normal part of life.

"Did you find him last night?"

Tie gripped in his hand, he asks coldly, "No, why?"

"I heard you talking about him during that meeting..." He gives me a sharp look and I know I've somehow made a mistake. I lick my lips nervously before explaining. "I wouldn't be upset... it would just be nice to know..."

How do I even say this?

"Know what, Lily?" he asks impatiently, taking a step towards me, his tie gripped in his fist.

Pressing back against the door, I consider my words carefully. My pulse is racing so fast I feel sick, and I know I'm not feeling sick for the right reasons.

"What do you want to know?" Lucifer presses, closing the distance between us.

I take a deep breath and can't believe I am actually going to say this. I'm an awful, horrible human being, but, "It would be nice to know if I'm a widow or not. It would save me a lot of paperwork."

Lucifer blinks at me as if I surprised him and then he's grinning. Leaning over me, he chuckles. "No, I haven't made you a widow."

I open my mouth, meaning to say something but he talks over me.

"In fact, you will never be Marshall's widow. I've taken care of that."

I frown at him now. Totally not following. "You mean Marshall is under your protection or something?"

"Absolutely not." His eyes flash with menace. "I've taken care of all the paperwork for you. You and Marshall are no longer married."

"What?" I ask stupefied. I don't think I heard him right. There's no way he could do something like that.

"You and Marshall are officially divorced, and the judge, *my* judge, has granted you full custody."

"But I don't remember signing anything? Wouldn't I have to go to court to do that?"

"What part of *I took care of it all for you* are you not comprehending?" he asks, caging me in with his arms like he's afraid I'm going to bolt or something.

Don't get me wrong, I don't want to be married to Marshall. Even before he proved himself to be an irredeemable scumbag that would trade away his own children I was planning on divorcing him.

But I should get a say in this. It should be something I get to do myself. I'd like to sign that paperwork myself, with flourish.

"You had no right." I frown up at him angrily. If he's telling the truth, and I'm very afraid he has managed to do this, it's yet another thing he's taken away from me.

"I have every right," Lucifer glares down at me.

"No…" I shake my head.

"Yes," he snaps. "I have every right because you are mine. And I had to, in order for us to be legally married. I won't let something pesky like the law get between us."

"Don't think for one second I want to marry you now! How could I after you did that?"

"It's too late, Lily," he grins as if he's enjoying this or something.

I suck in a shrill gasp. He can't be saying what I think he is saying. "What do you mean?"

"We're already married."

"When?!"

"As of today."

"No," I shake my head in denial. Am I still dreaming? "There are vows, and things to sign… and a priest for Christ sakes!"

"We'll have a ceremony for our friends and family this spring. In fact, you should probably start planning it."

"But…" I gape at him.

"No buts, Lily. On paper we're legally married and no judge in this state will overturn it."

"You can't get away with this. There's no way this is legal."

"The method may not be legal but the final product is."

I keep shaking my head and he keeps grinning. And then it just hits me, it completely sinks in. He did it, he really did it. Without my permission, without my consent, he divorced me from my husband and married me to him.

"I can't believe you!" I scream and try to shove him away. "How dare you. You had no right."

Face going cold, Lucifer grabs my hands, easily fighting me off as I try to slap him and pulls them up, pinning them above my head. "I have every right, Lily, because you are mine, and I take care of what's mine. It's time to accept it now, *you belong to me.* No more fucking games."

"You're horrible, you're despicable," I spit back.

He nods his head. "I am a not a good man. I will never deny it. Some of us are just destined to be bad men."

I open my mouth and his finger presses against my lips to stop me. "But you can count on me to take care of you. You can count on me to always do what is best for you, even if you don't see it that way. Even if you don't understand how it's in your best interest."

Leaning into me, his eyes lock on mine, not letting me look away. "I protect what's mine, and I will let nothing, not the law, not other men, not God his fucking self, come between me and my family. I will do everything in my power to protect you and our children. I will kill for you. I will die for you. And I will break the law for you as long as you are taken care of in the end. Do you understand?"

Staring into his eyes, I feel all the fight just go out of me and sag within his grip. Why keep fighting him? Why keep fighting this? He's offering my everything I could ever want.

Protection, security. Passion.

Everything but a choice.

Pulling his finger away from my lips he asks, "Lily? *Do you understand?*"

Tears blur my eyes as I struggle to accept it.

All I have to do is let go. All I have to do is hand over the power.

To be weak.

To put all my trust in him.

I'm never getting out of this. There will never be an opportunity for me to make off with the children. There's always someone around to stop us.

Do I even want to run anymore?

Maybe it's time I just close my eyes and jump off the cliff.

Maybe it's time to stop fighting this.

"Lily," he growls, his fingers pinching me with his impatience.

Taking a deep breath, I continue to look him in the eyes as I exhale, "Yes."

Sighing, he closes his eyes for a moment.

If he's willing to die for us, to kill for us, how bad of a

man can he be? Yes, there's blood on him, but there can be many justifiable reasons for it...

Eyes popping back open, he takes a step back and frowns at me. "Look what you made me do."

I look down at myself and see that the blood on his shirt has seeped into my blouse and has stained me too.

"Come," he says, pulling me by the hand. "Let's get washed up. I've missed you."

21

LUCIFER

This parenting stuff isn't too hard or bad.

Evie is racing around the living room chasing after Adam as she tries to brush his head. The squealing isn't the greatest of sounds but it beats the silence that filled this home before they came.

It's odd when I think about the changes I have made since I took Lily as mine and took on our children. To say I was in a different stage of my life before them would be putting it mildly. I had nothing but work, wanton women, and booze.

It wasn't a bad life, but it wasn't as satisfying as it is now.

I truly don't think Lily understood when I took them I was not doing this on a whim, they wouldn't be cast aside as soon as I grew bored. No, I have taken them on as mine, for good or bad they will be with me until our ends.

While she didn't understand that at first, I think the ending of her old marriage and the start of ours proved to her she wasn't just a passing whim. Fuck, how could she still think that? She's mine and I am hers.

Something primal is ripped from its dormancy when I see her, I can't be without her.

I can't live without dominating her, claiming her as mine and keeping her.

Never have I felt what I do when I look at her, never. She's a drug, a seductress…a need. In life there are wants and needs. Wants, you can live without, but needs are what you must have if you want to live.

"Father!" Adam yells out as he keeps running from a giggling Evie. "Tell her to stop, I'm not a girl!"

Laughing, I reach out as Evie tries to race past me, snatching her up into my arms. I hug her tight before giving her a kiss on her head. "Little princess, please stop torturing your brother. He's not a dollie."

Staring at me with a big smile, she looks from me to Adam. "He's pretty like you, Daddy!"

Grumbling, I set her down and tell her, "Go get Paul dear, tell him it's tea party time."

The phone in my pocket rings twice before I'm able to pull it out. Simon's name comes across the screen as I pick it up.

I watch as Evie screeches out of the room, belting out Paul's name.

"Hello Simon."

"Boss, where's Lilly? Where's Bart?"

"What's wrong?" I snap out of my joy as I quickly stand.

"Where are they Lucifer? Quickly."

"They are out shopping for wedding stuff. I think she said dresses."

It's been two weeks since I told her of our marriage license. It took a couple of days for her to come to terms with the whole thing. Now she's trying to break the damn card I gave her.

"Bart was their inside man. He was giving information over to the Yakuza. We need to get her away from him as soon as possible."

"What the fuck, Simon... How the fuck did you not see it?" I breathe out as my heart drops deep down in my chest.

Down where there is a rolling pit of nausea and rage ready to erupt.

"Not the time, boss. Does she still have the phone I gave you for her?"

"Yes."

"Okay, I need to start up the tracking, but I have a feeling Bart got rid of it as well as his."

My anger is clouding my vision as I track down James in the operations wing of my compound.

Snapping my fingers, I say, "James, you and Paul are on the children. If anyone but me or Lily come for them you are to shoot to kill. Do you understand my orders?"

He stares at me for a long moment before nodding his head. "I understand. Do you want me to take them into the safe room?"

Thinking quickly, I nod my head. "Yeah, get them all the toys and games you can. Fresh food. Have Mary help you pack up enough to occupy them for a couple of days just in case. Then, as soon as you are ready to go into the room, have her go home."

Standing up, he shoves his gun from the rack into his shoulder holster. "Anything else, sir?"

"No, get moving."

He heads out of the room, pulling his phone from his pocket and dialing quickly. "Paul, get Evie and meet me at the safe room. I'll get Adam."

Walking over to the gun rack, I start talking to Simon again. "Where are you?"

"Thaddeus, Phillip and I are on our way over to you now. John is heading over to the Jap's main stronghold off of third. From the video feed on the buildings, I haven't seen them bring her in, but I have no doubts she will be there soon."

"Get here now. We will be doing a full tactical load out from here, then we're heading down to them."

"Matthew, wait a minute. We need to make…"

At that moment, I can no longer contain my anger. "Silence!" comes bellowing from my mouth.

"Get. Here. Now." I say into the silent air.

"Seven minutes out," he says and disconnects the call.

Dropping the phone to the shelf, I take only a moment to assess what I need. Then I start by strapping a thigh holster on top of my jeans. Pulling the bulletproof tactical vest off of the rack, I start to adjust it for myself, shoving magazines in the slots as I go.

I hear shouting and running footsteps as I go through the rack, pulling my favored M4 tactical assault rifle out. Looking through the sighting, I load a clip into it, slapping it home. I check to make sure it's secured.

Turning to Simon, he's slowing down from a sprint as he heads straight to the weapons racks, gathering the things that he needs.

"The phone wasn't removed from her. Bart must not have known about it. She's being held in that shit office building on third. It's a two-story job. Legit business in the front, all illegal operations in the back. I've got the phone now reversed into being a microphone, broadcasting to us anything that it can hear."

I watch as the rest of the men swarm in, grabbing gear and weapons.

The Yakuza fucked up when they took in Marshall and thought to go against me. Now they have touched my fucking property.

Every single one of them will die.

## 22

LILY

There's freedom in giving in. In letting go. It took me a couple of days to fully come to terms with my new life, and my new situation. But after some deep soul searching, and a lot of thinking, I feel better about everything now.

I'm not sure this is something I would have chosen for myself or for my children, but when considering the alternatives, I can't imagine seeking out something different.

Is there anything better out there for us? Is there anyone better? I don't think so.

Lucifer didn't have to marry me. He didn't have to legally bind himself to me or take on the obligation of providing for my children. He could have let things continue to progress as they were. He could have stuck with the status quo. It's more in my best interest to be legally recognized as his wife now. To have the protection of his name and a right to his home.

He's given me more power by showing the world he thinks of me as someone more than a thing he just owns.

I can't think of a good reason to leave, and I can't think of any place I'd rather go.

For better or worse, this is my life now, this is my world.

I accept it all now.

I feel happier, I'm fulfilled. I didn't even realize how empty I was. How lost I was before he walked into my bedroom.

Haven't I always needed someone like him? It feels like I've been waiting for him. Waiting for someone to wake me up.

Waiting for someone to make me whole.

My entire future is ahead of me, and I'm excited about all these new changes. There are possibilities where there were none before.

Today, I've spent the entire day with one of my closest friends, Lisa, shopping for dresses. It's been a day just for us girls.

When I first reached out to her a couple of days ago, she was a little shocked about everything that has gone down since we last hung out, but even she was ecstatic to learn that I finally left Marshall.

Whether she's completely onboard with me marrying again so soon is to be seen, but like a true friend she's been more than happy to help me shop and plan for my upcoming nuptials.

We've shopped our way up and down Wedding Row. I have almost a dozen dresses ordered and picked out to try on for when my mother arrives next week. Everything is falling into place, and Lucifer's deep pockets are ensuring everything continues to progress smoothly.

I'm a little nervous about my parents flying in to visit, but

Lucifer is so charming I'm sure they'll have no trouble accepting him as their new son-in-law.

After hugging Lisa goodbye, Bart, my driver for the day, opens the back door of the car for me and I slide in, exhausted. Who knew picking out dresses would take so long?

Settling into the backseat, I whip out my phone and notice I have a text from my mom. She's just dying to know what dresses I've picked out, and she can't wait until next week to see me try them on.

Texting her back, I'm vaguely aware of Bart receiving a phone call as we pull out, but honestly, I don't pay much attention to it. The guys Lucifer assigns to me are always receiving calls and texts when we're out, and I just assume they're receiving instructions or someone is checking up on where we are.

After listing all the designers for my mom, I peek my head up and glance out the window. I don't recognize the area we're driving through but assume Bart is just taking a short cut.

I spend a few more moments texting back and forth with my mom before saying goodbye to her. Clicking off my phone, I slip it into the pocket of my sweater and lean back against the seat, closing my eyes and starting to doze.

It's not until we pull up in front of a run-down looking building that I get the hint that something is wrong. Opening my eyes, I peer out the window and wonder why we're slowing down.

"Bart?" I ask, leaning forward. "Why are we here? I'm done shopping and would like to go home now."

Bart parks the car and doesn't say a word. He won't even meet my eyes in the rearview mirror.

"Hey? Earth to Bart?" I frown in frustration and then my door flies open.

"What the hell?!" I cry out as a hand reaches in and yanks me out by the arm.

I stumble and then I'm thrown down. My knees hit the asphalt hard.

"Careful with the goods, idiot!" A sharp voice calls out.

My knees throbbing with pain, I cry out as someone grabs me by the hair and yanks my head back.

"I was told to rough her up a little," a deep voice rumbles.

My head is held at an incredibly painful angle and all I can see above me is a darkening sky.

"This her?"

Reaching up, I claw and pull desperately at the hand yanking on my hair.

"Yes," the first voice confirms. "Let's get her inside before she starts drawing attention."

The fingers in my hair loosen and my head falls forward. My scalp is throbbing and stinging with pain. I can't see shit because my eyes are overflowing with tears.

Sucking in a mouthful of air, I open up my mouth to let out a scream but a hand slaps against my mouth.

My scream is muffled against a sweaty palm.

A beefy arm goes around my middle, trapping my arms, and I'm hauled up. I kick out, connecting with some shins, and whoever is holding me curses in my ear.

"Can I knock her out?"

"No. He needs her awake to interrogate her. We don't have much time."

I twist and I kick as I'm dragged backward. I don't know where they're taking me but I know I don't want to go. My phone is still in my pocket. If I can get free for just a minute, I can call Lucifer for help.

"If you don't fucking stop I'm going to break your legs," the deep voice warns.

Fuck him if he thinks he can scare me into obeying. I kick back even harder wishing I could reach his nuts.

"Need some help?" the first voice chuckles.

"Yes," the man holding me huffs.

I watch as the first man comes into view. I don't know who he is but the sight of him chills my blood. He's Asian, Japanese perhaps.

With a feral grin he reaches for me and I don't know why I notice it but part of the little finger on his right hand looks like it was cut off.

Grabbing my legs and lifting them up, his grin only grows wider as I continue to twist and fight, screaming at him against the hand covering my mouth.

"She's a feisty little one, isn't she?"

The guy behind me only grunts.

Eyes meeting my eyes, I know he's purposely trying to freak me out when he says, "We're going to have a lot of fun when the interrogation is done."

Despite my struggles, the two holding me manage to carry me into a building and then down a flight of rickety stairs without dropping me to the ground.

I'm dumped into a chair and held down while I'm secured to it with a long length of rope. The sweaty palm pulls away only to be replaced by a gag made out of dusty cloth.

Drained after all of my struggles, I push and wiggle against the rope but it holds.

The two men who carried me step away and a new, older, elderly Asian man steps forward. He says something in Japanese I don't understand.

"Fuck, you didn't say anything about her being pregnant," the man who carried my legs says accusingly to someone behind me.

Pregnant? I'm not pregnant. I just had my period…

Shit.

"How the fuck was I to know?" Marshall says. "After the last one wrecked her pussy, I thought she was barren."

Walking around my chair, Marshall comes to stand in front of me with a look of triumph on his pale pudgy face. "Hello, Lily."

Snarling against the gag, I glare murderously at my ex-husband and fight against my ropes. He's dead if I get my hands on him.

The older man says something in Japanese again.

The younger one translates, "It's going to affect her price on the market considerably."

"Not many want to have a go at dumpy hag with a bun in the oven, eh?"

The older man laughs and the younger one shakes his head. There's some back and forth between the two in Japanese before the younger one nods his head. Turning back to Marshall he says, "We're prepared to offer you twice your asking price, as long as her condition remains."

Marshall seems to mull that over. Making a great show of tapping his chin and furrowing his brow. "Well, I suppose I can go easy on her... as long as she tells me what I want to know."

The younger man nods. "It would be worth your while."

With a great sigh Marshall's hand drops from his chin and he nods back at the other man.

Their business done, Marshall takes a step forward and drops down to a squat, putting us at eye level.

"I'm going to remove your gag. If you scream, I'm going to punch out your teeth."

Reaching around me, he unties my gag and I spit it out of my mouth.

Tongue dry, I press my lips together as Marshall grabs me by the back of the head. Tugging on my hair, I cry out as my scalp lights up with renewed pain.

What the fuck is up with these guys and all the hair pulling?

"One question. All you have to do is answer one question, Lily, and we'll be done here. You'll never see me again."

Panting through the pain, I stare into his eyes, showing him I'm not afraid of him. "You're going to die for this."

"I haven't asked the question yet, bitch."

He pulls on my hair again, and my scalp is so abused, so raw, it takes every ounce of strength I have not to scream. Not because I'm afraid of him punching out my teeth, but because I just don't want to give him the satisfaction.

Breathing through the pain, he waits for my pants to quiet before he's staring into my eyes again. "Are you ready for your question?"

I don't answer him at first so he tugs on my hair again.

Gritting my teeth together, I grind out, "Yes."

"Good," he grins. "Now, all you have to do is tell me where the family portrait that was hanging over the fireplace is, and we can be done with all of this."

Is he serious? He can't be serious?

"Where is it?" he hisses and tugs on my hair.

Dammit it all, my scalp is so raw I'm really close to screaming. "What portrait?" I hiss, buying time.

"The one that was hanging over the fireplace, you stupid bitch."

"Oh, that one…Why do you want it?"

He yanks on my hair, hard, and this time I scream. I just can't help it. It feels like my scalp is detaching from my head. "I'm the one asking the questions."

"Tell me why and I'll tell you where it is," I cry out.

He pulls on my hair some more but all I do is scream.

Finally, when he realizes he's not going to get an answer out of me like this, he relents.

I hear some rapid Japanese being spoken but I still don't understand it or get the gist.

"My grandfather is not pleased with the amount of stress you are causing. If she loses the baby we will drop the price."

"Fine, fuck. I'll stop. Don't drop the price."

Pulling his fingers from my hair, Marshall drops the chunks he's pulled out to the floor.

Shaking his hand, he tries to shake off the strands that have wrapped around his knuckles while he tells me, "I've written the numbers for my offshore accounts on the back of it. Happy? Now tell me where the fuck it is."

I can't help it. It's just too perfect. Even though my head is pounding like mad, I can't stop my head from tipping back. I can't stop the laughs that come bubbling up.

"What the fuck is so funny?" Marshall demands.

I have to suck in a big breath to even tell him, "It's in the trash!"

"What?!" he snarls. "What do you mean it's in the trash?"

"It's gone!" I gasp and bend forward, straining against my rope as I struggle to catch my breath. "Just like our marriage, broken and thrown away."

"You stupid bitch!" Marshall roars and I don't even see his fist coming, it just pounds into me.

## 23

LUCIFER

*R*age and anger are the things that can make a man stupid, lead him to make mistakes. But it can also galvanize.

I can't afford to be stupid now. Not when so much is on the line.

I don't know what Simon had to do on Lily's phone but I am thankful for what it's doing. I am able to hear now everything that is being said, even if I have to bear through the screams.

They have hurt Lily, and it's her screams that hurt me the most. She is in this position because of two soon to be dead men. Bart will die, if I find him he dies. Hearing Marshall's voice makes my blood fucking boil.

"Where is the fucking family portrait!?!" Marshall bellows out.

I hear more scuffling then I hear a female grunt painfully as she tries to gasp in air. The motherfucker is hitting her, I know it. I hear a loud slap of skin on skin as I can only imagine him hitting her like the little bitch he is.

Looking up ahead of me, Andrew is driving at a near reckless pace, but he keeps control of the wheel as we race to where they are holding Lily.

"Simon. Where are we with all our guys?" I ask.

"Word is completely out to all men, converge on location. Snipers will be in position within five minutes." Tilting his head to the side, he holds his phone tight to his ear. Then smiling, he looks over at me. "Fake officer down call has just been put out across the city. All police districts will be busy soon, the one we will be in will have a riot started at its outer edge.

Nodding, I pull my pistol from the thigh holster. "I want this location locked down tight. I don't give a fuck if the national guard is called in, no one comes into the district until we are finished."

"One sec," says Simon into his phone as he switches to the other line. "Marco, it's good to speak with…"

"Two minutes from location," Andrew says over his shoulder.

"Where are we coming in at?"

"Straight from the front," Andrew says and looks over to Simon who nods.

Putting his phone down, Simon disconnects the call to look at me. "Everything's a go on our side. Marco has heard of our issue. The fucking Japs are spreading it all over the city that they are fucking around with you. They think they have the edge. Marco has decided to push at every single place he can. He is taking on the Yakuza in a big way, no paybacks expected."

"Good, he can have every single fucking business or front they have as soon as this is over. We will assist in every way, have them fully removed."

"This should cut the head off of the snake, Lucifer. Anything that's left won't be much."

"They will more than likely go to the Russians for a refuge..." Simon says.

"Call Vladimir. One million to them if they bring me fifteen heads from the Yakuza."

"Jesus... Lucifer..."

Turning my gaze from the road ahead, I say, "Is there a problem, Simon?"

He looks at me for a very long time, and I don't doubt he is questioning my thoroughness. "Are you sure you want to go this far?"

"They took something that is mine, Simon."

"Fuck, do you love her?"

"Of course."

"Alright, I'll tell them, but you know how fucking crazy the Russians are. They are going to most likely bring the heads to you. Like literally."

Grinning, I say, "Good, I'll fucking send them on to the bosses back in Japan."

We slow down as we roll through the Japanese section of the city. It looks like the streets have cleared themselves after they've seen all the cars of my men rolling through. I doubt any of my guys have bothered to hide all the weaponry they are bringing to the fight.

"Snipers in place. Back, front and sides are all covered. We have men down the street as well, in all directions, looking for hidden exfiltration sites."

Stopping in front of the building, I wait until Andrew hops out with his AK aimed at the front of the small grocery store. Stepping from the vehicle, I pull my M4 to my front and begin to stalk into the store directly behind Andrew.

I've never served in the military, never been in the police. All my training and expertise has come from the men I have employed. They are who keep me alive, and I them. Andrew, though, was former special teams, and so were most of the men I have surrounding me.

Walking through the doors we are instantly on the offensive as a long burst of machine gun fire erupts from the back of the store, exploding glass and dry goods all around us. The man shooting at us, though, is obviously untrained in any form of shooting discipline as he wasted a whole clip of bullets to hit nothing but shit.

Sticking up from his crouch, Andrew fires three rapid shots. No doubt the thump I hear is the body of the guy shooting at us hitting the floor.

"Moving!" Andrew shouts over his shoulder as he advances.

I'm directly behind him, watching his angles.

I hear Simon bitch loudly from behind. "Fucking hell. They put a hole through my fucking coat."

A man pops up from the back and I put a bullet through his throat before one from a man behind me makes his head explode.

"Snipers reporting from the back, we have them pinned down. Sending group D to bring heavy fire on them," Simon yells to me.

Nodding my head, I yell, "Move forward!"

It's a slow, steady march towards the back of the store. Sending groups up and to the sides to eliminate any surprises takes more time than I am comfortable with, but it's unavoidable. Bodies are beginning to stack up from all the men they have sent to defend against us.

Once we reach the main door to the back, I look back to Simon. "How are we on a police presence?"

"Not on the radar, for the moment, but I don't know if that can hold forever. We need to quiet this down quickly."

Putting my gun to work as we make it through their small

dock station, I watch as the men trying to escape through the back are gunned down immediately. A lone old man stands completely still, thrusting his hands in the air.

"Where is the girl?" I yell at him in Japanese. Raising my hand, I backhand him as hard as I can. Flying to the ground, he sputters as he points to a door off to the side. It has a small sign reading *Basement* on it.

Throughout all the gunfire my earpiece has been bursting with men yelling in Japanese as they tried to muster a defense against our onslaught. They only begin to panic as they figure out that they are now surrounded from above. From what I can hear, the men speaking in rapid fire sentences don't have an exit.

Walking to the door, I kick it in as I yell, "Drop your weapons. All of you."

Screaming out my name, I hear Lily, "Lucifer!"

There is a loud rattle of metal weapons hitting the bottom of the stairs, but from the earpiece I hear them say, "Drop a bunch, but as soon as they come down start shooting. We can try and get Lucifer."

"Start coming up one by one. If I have to come get you, you die."

"Fuck." Men mutter in Japanese and English.

"No way guys, kill this fucker!" Marshal starts to plead with the men around him. He sounds like he is on the verge of tears.

"Shut the fuck up, pussy! This is all your fault!" Bart yells at him.

My smile is slowly growing wider. The stupid fucks aren't even going to put up a fight with us when they come up. It's my turn to play.

Each man slowly comes up the stairs. Quickly frisked, they are lined up.

Looking over to Simon, I say, "Pull all teams back

except those watching out for the police. Any Yakuza wandering around the city are to be rounded up. Ten-thousand-dollar reward per one, but they must be proven Yakuza."

Bart and Marshall are the last two left down in the room. Motioning Andrew to follow me, I stop the train of men on the stairs and head down. I hear Simon moving the guys once we are past to keep the prisoners in check.

Bart is against the wall in the basement, his hands down, hanging empty at his sides. Marshall is standing next to Lily with a gun to her temple.

"Hello, love," I say looking into her eyes. She is so beautiful even now, beaten and bruised, her eyes shine to me.

"Shu…Shut the fuck …Up." Marshall stutters. "I want… I want out of here or she… dies."

Andrew looks from me to Marshall. "You want me to kill him, sir? Or do you?"

"I have him."

"Good, I want Bart all to myself then." He grins as he motions to Bart to turn around.

Looking at Marshall, I walk toward him and Lily. "Give me the pistol, Marshall."

His hand is shaking as he tells me, "No!"

I take the last step before I strike out for him with the side of my pistol. Connecting with his temple, I watch as his body crumples to the ground.

Leaning down, I untie Lily's ropes and pull her up to my chest. Her head rests on me as she sobs quietly.

I hear Andrew in the background using a zip tie. Turning us to face them, I watch Andrew pull Bart away from the wall then escort him up the stairs.

Andrew is a rare breed of man. His loyalty is absolute, as is his desire to seek vengeance on any who touch those he works for.

I shout up the stairs, "James, come down to bring Marshall up."

Lifting Lily up into a threshold carry, I take her up the stairs and out of the store to the waiting SUV.

Pulling the door closed on us, I wait as Simon comes up to the window. "What should we do with them all?"

"I want all survivors brought to the warehouse. Have men there to set it up for us."

"Yes, sir."

Thaddeus climbs into the front seat and looks back. "Andrew has requested to be the one to deal with Bart."

Thinking for a moment, I frown. Bart should truly be punished by me. But as I said, Andrew doesn't take kindly to traitors.

"That's fine, let's move."

∼

I CAN'T LET her away from me again. Not any time soon. My arm is wrapped around Lily's shoulders as I lead her into the warehouse. First through the front office, then through the workshop. Finally, we come to the backroom.

"What are we doing, Lucifer?" she asks quietly as she sees all our captives standing in a lineup with my men surrounding them.

"Point out each man that touched you, Lily," I say as I hold her firmly next to me.

"Wha... Why?"

"They can't touch you and get away with it. No one can."

She doesn't stop looking up into my eyes for a long time. Hers are so deep and so vulnerable right now that it makes me even more angry that someone has put her in such a position.

Slowly, she looks from me to each man. Ten are standing

there. Pointing to five of them she says, "That's them.... But Bart... he's not here."

I explain, "Andrew is taking care of him."

"Oh, okay."

Nodding to James, I say, "You saw which ones, take the rest outside and shoot the fucks. Leave the old fuckhead."

Lily gasps beside me. "But..."

"This is war Lily; it was them or us."

Pulling away from her, I walk over to the four men who dared touch my wife. "Every single male member of your family in America will be dead before the week is out. Every woman will be sold into slavery in Africa. Your children will be sent to their deaths. I promise you your families in Japan will die soon as well. Your bloodlines are going to be erased from the planet. Fuck shaming them, I will erase you all."

Pulling my pistol out from my holster, I motion for my men to get to work. It's a quick affair as the four men die instantly from multiple bullet wounds.

Behind me I hear Lily gasp. "Lucifer!"

Turning to her, I shake my head. "They will learn to fear my name even in Japan now."

I point to Marshall who is pulled over to a wooden chair that once had a wicker seat attached to it. Now it's only a frame of a chair, just enough left to keep his fat ass from falling through it. "Strip him and strap him down."

Removing my coat, I walk over to a small table. Pulling off my holster, I set it and the coat down. The pistol right on top of it.

Turning back to my men as they finish up, I say, "Leave us."

Lily watches in shocked silence as everyone leaves the room except for her, Marshall and I.

Smiling at her, I walk over to kiss her brow. "It's almost over my dear, Lily. He is the last one to die now."

Grabbing the long length of metal chain from the table, I grin at Marshall. He is gagged and screaming violently into the cloth but I can't make out his words. No matter. "It's time for pain, Marshall."

Swinging the chain, I swing it up, under the seat where it connects with the exposed dangling parts of his small anatomy. Fucker has some big balls for such a tiny little prick.

The scream is audible through the gag, though, unlike earlier. I must have hit a testicle on that one.

Laughing, I say, "I haven't done this before. I wasn't sure I'd have the aim down…"

I swing again and feel a solid connection to his body. I don't think I hit the right spot though.

I do it twice more before I say, "I heard what you said in the room to her, Marshall. I heard about your plans of selling her into slavery. I heard your plans to sell my unborn child. I heard it all."

Dropping the chain, I head back to the table. Pulling a blowtorch down I start to strike it up. I want to melt something badly right now.

"You said you would sell her, Marshall, as if she was yours to do with as you liked. *She's mine!*"

Walking over to him, I position myself behind his chair and aim the torch at his fingers.

The smell is enough to make me heave, but his screams help settle my stomach.

## 24

LILY

Four unarmed men were just gunned down in front of me and no one batted an eye. Not a single one of Lucifer's men seemed to blink. It was all carried out so efficiently, so quickly, like they've done this numerous times before…

That thought alone is enough to make my blood run cold. I know Lucifer is a 'bad man' but I didn't quite comprehend the scope of it until now. Automatic weapons. A full tactical outfit. His own personal army to carry out his will. How many have died today? How many still will?

*Every woman will be sold into slavery in Africa. Your children will be sent to their deaths. I promise you your families in Japan will die soon as well.*

Was he telling the truth or was that all for show?

I feel like I've been ripped from one nightmare only to be thrust into another. My world has been flipped upside down.

Is this real? Is this really happening? Or have I died and gone to hell?

*The smell.*

If it wasn't for the smell of Marshall's flesh burning I could perhaps convince myself none of this is real.

I'd like nothing more than to curl up into a little ball and crawl back into my comfortable shell. Pretend I didn't see this. Pretend it was all some kind of nightmare. Just a bad dream…

But I can't.

The smell. Oh, god, the smell.

Marshall is screaming, and Lucifer's eyes are laughing. I've never seen someone take so much pleasure in another's suffering. It's as if he's actually enjoying this, he's getting off on what he's doing to Marshall somehow.

"Stop!" I'm screaming. I can't actually see what Lucifer is doing behind Marshall's chair but I know it must be awful.

How? How can he do it? Doesn't he have a fucking soul?

"No, my love, I will not stop. He must pay for what he did to you and our unborn child."

Lucifer's arms move and I imagine him swiping the blowtorch in a swath across Marshall's back.

There's this wild panic welling up inside me. I can't stop shaking. I can't stop the floor from shifting beneath my feet. The world is spinning out of control.

Still, I manage to take one step forward then another.

I have to stop this. I have to.

Hand covering my nose, it's not enough to block out the smell but it helps. Heaving, I gag and somehow keep what little is in my stomach down.

I can't afford to be sick. My head hurts so bad it actually helps to keep the nausea back.

It takes so much effort to move, gravity itself is fighting

against me. Walking right now is like trying to run underwater.

Stumbling forward, I grab onto the edge of a small table and steady myself.

Marshall keeps screaming and begging behind his gag. As much as I personally detest the man I can't just stand here and watch him suffer like this. It's unthinkable.

It's completely unbearable.

My entire being is in turmoil. I can't think straight. My eyes can't focus. There's this cold horror rattling my bones.

With a shaky hand, I pick up the pistol Lucifer left lying on the table.

"Stop," I cry out but my voice sounds so small, so uncertain.

Lucifer looks up at me and makes a tsking sound of disapproval. "Put the gun down, Lily."

Lifting my chin into the air, the gun is shaking in my hand and I'm trying to be brave but then it goes off.

Lucifer's eyes go as wide as mine.

Shit, I totally didn't mean to do that, but I don't let him know that. I ease my finger away from the trigger as he switches the blowtorch off.

Marshall slumps forward in his bonds, dead or passed out.

Is it over? That horrible panicked thing inside me begins to settle down.

Lucifer stares at me for the longest time.

"Fine. You don't like the blowtorch," he finally shrugs and sets the blowtorch down on the table next to Marshall. "It's not my favorite either. The smell is fucking horrible."

Now that the blowtorch is out of the picture, I begin to relax. I point the gun down, towards the floor.

"I'll have to call Rosa and tell her to take the bacon off

tomorrow's menu," he says before grabbing something on the other side of Marshall's chair by the handle.

Before I can fully process what's about to happen, Lucifer walks around the front of Marshall's chair and heaves up a sledgehammer. Leaning back, he takes aim then swings it forward. The sledgehammer collides with Marshall's knees with a loud crack.

Marshall comes to, screaming out in agony.

Lucifer's eyes gleam with pure, unadulterated pleasure.

"What the fuck," I gasp, lifting the gun and pointing it at Lucifer's head. "What the actual fuck?"

The pleasure dims in Lucifer's eyes as he glances over at me and more pointedly the gun aimed at his head. "What? Too much?"

I shake my head in disbelief. "What the fuck is wrong with you?"

He looks me dead in the eyes as he says, "He touched you."

I don't even know what to say to that.

Lifting the sledgehammer again, he weighs it thoughtfully in his hands. "He put you in danger."

Taking a step back, I watch him line up with Marshall's knees. I know I should stop him but I can't quite bring myself to do it.

Everything is spinning out of control. I don't know what to do. Should I shoot? Who do I shoot?

How did it all come to this?

Swinging forward, the sledgehammer crashes into Marshall again while Lucifer roars above the crack, "He fucking hurt you!"

Marshall blubbers and begs behind his gag. He's such a mess from the thigh down I can't even bear to look at him.

"Stop, please. You have to stop," I beg willing my hand to stop shaking. Averting my eyes, I focus on the pools of blood on the floor instead, finding a strange calm in them. "It's enough. You've done enough. *Please.*"

"It will never be enough, Lily. He deserves so much more than I could ever do to him."

"No," I shake my head, unable to keep the tears back. "No one deserves this. No one."

"You only say that because you don't know what he had planned for the children."

And just like that the edges of my vision stop shaking. Everything comes into sharp focus.

"What?" I ask, glancing back up in shock. "What are you talking about?"

Still gripping the sledgehammer in his hands, Lucifer turns towards me, his face a cold mask.

"I heard them talking in Japanese. You may not have understood what they were saying but I did. I'm fluent. You think he was going to stop with you once he got what he wanted? No. He also made a deal to sell the children. The Yakuza were especially interested in Adam… they had a Middle Eastern buyer lined up, prepared to pay top dollar."

"Oh god," I gasp, feeling a fresh wave of bile rising up in my throat.

"And our little Evie with her blonde hair…"

Every ounce of compassion I was feeling for Marshall goes up in flames in an instant. He was going to hurt my children? My babies?

I turn the gun now on Marshall. "You fucking monster! You were going to sell the children too?"

I don't need his answer. Of course he was. After he gave us to Lucifer, how could I expect anything less?

"Don't shoot him, my love. A bullet would be too gentle."

Marshall moans and shakes his head weakly back and forth. My finger brushes against the trigger. Everything in me wants to shoot him, to put an end to this.

But I just can't bring myself to do it.

How do I end a life? Even his? He's done awful, horrible things to us. He's the entire reason the children and I are even in this mess. I would never have been in this position if he had just stepped up. If he had given a shit. If he had been a husband, a father. If he had just been a fucking man.

"Lily…" Lucifer says softly, dropping the sledgehammer to the ground with a thud before he begins to walk towards me.

I turn towards him and the gun turns with me.

"Put the gun down," he says calmly.

I shake my head but I'm lowering the barrel down as I do it. If I can't shoot Marshall how can I shoot him? Now that I know why he's doing all of this I get it. I totally understand why he's doing this.

Gently, Lucifer lays his hand on top of the pistol and pushes it down. "Give me that," he says softly, drawing it from my fingers. Turning, he sets the pistol off to the side before pulling me into his arms.

I need his arms around me. I need his warmth and his comfort. Clutching his shirt, I bury my face against his chest and all the emotions inside of me come bubbling out of my mouth. I cry and I sob, soaking him with my tears. I cry for myself. For my children. For Marshall.

He holds me through it all, stroking back my hair and whispering soft words of comfort.

"It will all be over soon," Lucifer reassures me as my sobs die away.

The numbness is starting to sink in. I welcome it. I need it to get through this.

Tipping my head back, I peer up at his face. "Lucifer—"

His eyes flash and he cuts me off. "Use my name, Lily."

I lick my lips and say his name tentatively. It feels foreign and strange on my tongue. "Matthew… I want to go home. I want to see Adam and Evelyn."

He nods, tucking a stray strand of hair behind my ear. "We're almost done here."

I don't like the sound of that. What more is there to do? How much more can Marshall's body withstand?

"Can't you just shoot him like the others so we can get out of here?"

Did I really just say that?

"No. We must send a message. This kind of shit ends here. No one messes with you, and no one will after this."

"I don't know if I can…" I say, my voice quivering. I'm pretty sure I've reached my brutal torture limit.

Lucifer nods and turns with me, guiding me slowly to a chair. "You don't have to watch."

"Can't I just go home?" I ask hopefully.

"No," he says and pushes me down until I'm seated. "It will be a long time before I'll be able to let you out of sight again."

Oh god, he's really going to make me do this. He's going to make me sit here while he tortures Marshall behind my back.

"Not much longer, my love," he reassures me. "Then we can go home."

Squeezing my shoulder, he turns away and I listen to his footsteps as he walks away from me.

Staring forward, I focus on the concrete wall in front of me and try to block out what comes next.

Unfortunately, not being able to actually see what is happening only seems to amplify the sounds. Every grunt, every crack hits my ear in crystal clear high definition. I can only imagine what is happening, and I try very hard not to picture it.

There's the clanking of metal against metal, Marshall's cries and muffled begging, and worst of all Lucifer's laughs.

"Look what you made me do..." Lucifer chides Marshall and then Marshall starts screaming in earnest.

My hands shake and I clasp them together but then the rest of my body begins to shake and I break out in a cold sweat. I don't know how much time passes but my resolve begins to crumble.

I can't go along with this; I can't be a part of this.

Just as I rise from my chair, Marshall's screams rise in volume.

"He's almost done. Do you have any last words for him, Lily?"

I freeze in place, not daring to turn around. I know whatever is back there I don't want to see it.

A million things run through my mind. A million questions.

But the only one I can get past my lips is, "Why?"

Marshall coughs and sputters. I brace myself, waiting to hear... what? The final death blow? The absence of suffering?

I certainly don't expect Marshall to try to answer me after everything he's been through.

"Lily, I would never sell our—"

Whatever he was trying to say is cut off by a wet, smacking sound. Then he's only gurgling.

There's thrashing, skin slapping against skin.

Then it all quiets. The only thing I can hear is my own labored panting.

Is it done?

Is this it?

"He's gone," Lucifer grunts.

I'm suddenly overcome by the strongest wave of sadness. He's dead, he's really dead.

"Don't cry for him," Lucifer tells me, pulling me into his

arms. I didn't even hear him walk up over the noise of my sobs. "Don't waste your tears on him. He doesn't deserve them."

I'm not crying only for Marshall, though, I'm crying for all of us.

Lucifer lifts me up into his arms and carries me out of the torture room. I cling desperately to him, hiding my face against his shoulder and wrapping my arms around his neck.

"All done?" I recognize James' voice.

"Yes, have someone clean up the room," Lucifer answers.

"The body?"

"Save it. It's a message."

Lucifer's arms tighten around me and he hauls me back up as I start to slip down. "How are the children?"

"They're safe in the safe room. I've sent word but they won't release them until you personally see to it. Is she okay?"

"Yes. It's been a long day, she's exhausted."

Lucifer carries me out into the day. It's strange, it feels like so much has happened today that it should be night by now. That the things that happened in that room should have only happened in the darkness.

Cold air hits my back and the sunlight stings my eyes. I clench them shut and cling harder to his neck.

Someone wraps a coat around me. It isn't enough to keep the chill out of my bones but it helps.

A car door opens. We slide into warmth.

"Where to?"

"Home," Lucifer answers.

The car door shuts. We fall into a heavy silence.

As the car pulls out, I focus on Lucifer. The steady beat of his heart, the slow, even rate of his breathing.

After a few minutes, his arms tighten around me and I feel his lips against the top of my head. "I love you, Lily."

As broken as my heart is at this moment, it warms and swells to hear him say that.

"After this, no one will ever try to take you away from me again."

His arms tighten, nearly cracking my ribs.

"No one will try to hurt our children."

I gasp and my body shudders as I start sobbing again.

"Lily?" he asks and gently pushes me away. His fingers go to my chin and he tips my head up, forcing me to look at him.

Even through the blur of my tears, he's beautiful. A beautiful monster.

But he's my monster.

And despite everything… I love him.

EPILOGUE

LILY

9 MONTHS LATER

"It's a boy!" The doctor cries out triumphantly from between my knees.

My son's first cries of life are like music to my ears.

"You did so good," Matthew murmurs, peppering my face with kisses. "So good." He beams down at me, looking every inch the proud, happy father.

I smile weakly up at him.

I'm exhausted but happy that the pain is done. My labor was fast, faster than my previous two, but the most painful one yet.

It was worth it though, so worth it.

The past few months haven't always been easy, but Matthew has been by my side the whole way, and it feels like every day I fall more and more in love with him. He's so good to me, he treats me like a queen, and he's amazing with the kids. You can tell he loves them, really loves them.

And true to his word, after he sent his *message* there have been no more attempts on our family or his operations. We've been safe, happy, and prosperous.

There's a flurry of action at the end of my bed. The nurses whisk my son over to a little station that's been set up, taking his weight and vitals down while the doctor finishes up attending to me.

"How do you feel, Lilith?" The doctor asks, rolling away from my bed and standing from his stool. He pulls off his gloves and tosses them in the trash.

"I feel good, just tired."

The doctor nods. "That's to be expected. Everything looks good, but you should take it easy for a few days. Do you want something for the pain?"

I shake my head, "No."

Matthew says over me, "Yes."

I frown up at him.

He meets my glare and straightens from his bent position, now towering over the side of my bed. "Lily," he admonishes me.

"Fine," I sigh, giving in. I don't have the energy to fight over this. "I'll take something."

"Good," The doctor smiles, looking between us. "I'll write up the script and someone will be around shortly with it. Do you have any questions?"

We both shake our heads.

"Well, then," he steps forward, sticking out his hand. "Congratulations. I'll be around later to check in."

After shaking hands, we both say goodbye to my doctor and thank him. Then I wonder what's taking so long with the nurses.

Is something wrong? Did they find something? I can hear a bunch of chattering coming from the station, and my son is no longer crying, but they haven't returned him to me yet. It's crucial that my son and I start skin to skin contact.

After a couple more minutes pass I look up at Matthew. "What's taking so long?"

"I don't know," he frowns. "I'll go check."

Reluctantly peeling away from my side, Matthew walks to the back of the room and greets the nurses.

"Is everything alright?" I hear him ask.

"Oh yes, yes," the nurses reassure him and one of them giggles. "He's just so beautiful…"

"He's like a little angel," one of them sighs.

"In my twenty years working this ward, I've never seen a baby as cute as him."

I don't remember the nurses ever fawning over Adam or Evelyn this much after they were born. I have to wonder if these are actual nurses and not their younger, less experienced assistants.

I hear Matthew thank the ladies and then he asks if he can hold his son. Eagerly the nurses help him take our baby into his arms. Turning back to me, Matthew beams, walking carefully back to my bed.

Sitting up eagerly, I hold my arms out, accepting my little bundle. Matthew bends over me and we both gaze down at the little person we created.

"He's perfect," Matthew sighs and leans down, kissing first his head then my head.

"Yes," I softly agree with him.

Our eyes meet and we share a moment of pure contentment. Then Matthew nods at me and takes a step back.

Unwrapping the blanket he's been swaddled in, I take a moment to brush back my son's blonde, downy hair and then I bring him up to my breast.

He latches without hesitation.

"You sure about the name?" Matthew asks and it's obvious he still wants me to reconsider it.

We've been going back and forth on this but I'm putting my foot down. He, for whatever reason, wants to name our son Damian. I, on the other hand, would rather name him after my grandfather, David.

"Yes, I'm sure. I still like David best."

"Very well," he sighs as if it pains him to give in. "David it is."

"Thank you," I smile, happy and relieved I no longer have to fight him on this.

"You know I can always have it changed later…" he grins playfully.

"You wouldn't!" I gasp at him.

He chuckles and nods his head. "I wouldn't."

Little David nurses for some time and after a while the hormones start to kick in. Feeling incredibly sleepy, I start to drift off.

I jerk awake just as Matthew is lifting David away from my breast.

"Get some rest. I'll take care of him," he says softly.

I'm so tired all I can do is murmur my thanks, sinking down into the bed.

When I awake, the room is quiet, too quiet. Sitting up straight, I search for David or Matthew only to find Mary seated in the chair beside my bed.

"Good morning, dearie," she greets me. In her arms she holds David, swaddled up tightly in his blue blanket.

I start to relax. Over the past few months, I've come to trust her. She's picked up most of my slack with the children as I've grown bigger and less mobile. She's been absolutely amazing with them.

"Where's Matthew?" I ask, reaching for the little remote thing that will change the position of my mattress.

"Oh, he's off speaking to the hospital administration."

"Oh?"

She nods her head sharply. "Yes. He is not pleased. He wants you and little David discharged immediately."

"What? Why?" I ask in surprise as I finally find the remote and push the button that changes my position.

"The nurses keep sneaking in. He caught one of them taking a selfie with David without his permission."

My eyes widen and she nods her head knowingly. "They did the same when Matthew was born."

Rising from her chair, she walks over to the bed and offers David to me. I gratefully accept him and hug him to my chest.

"All the nurses and women went gaga over him. His father was the same, not at all pleased by the attention."

Gazing down at David, I admire his tiny little face. He is stunning with his soft, blonde hair and bright blue eyes. I feel that same pull, that same weakness I feel for his father.

Already I am so in love, there's nothing I wouldn't do for him.

"He's destined to be a killer just like his dear old dad," Mary says warmly.

My head jerks up and I blink at her. "Sorry? What did you say?"

Did I hear that right?

Mary frowns at me. "I said he's destined to be a lady killer just like his dear old dad. With that face, there will be few who will be able to resist him."

"Oh," I say. "I'm sorry, I must have misheard you."

Mary's frown turns into a smile and she pats my hand. "It's okay, dear. You've had a long day."

I smile at her, but still, I can't help but feel like I heard her correctly the first time…

THE END

PLAYLISTS

LUCIFER'S PLAYLIST

http://spoti.fi/2wd8Yhw

Christian Woman - Type O Negative
Lonesome Soul - The Color Morale
The Devil In I - Slipknot
Stranded - Gojira
Crows - The Plot In You
An Honorable Reign - Bury Tomorrow
Monster - Starset
More Human Than Human - White Zombie
A Match Made In Heaven - Architects

LILY'S PLAYLIST

http://spoti.fi/2eQe3K9
One Way Or Another - Until The Ribbon Breaks

Once Upon A Dream - Lana Del Ray
Raise The Dead - Rachel Rabin
Tainted Love - Claire Guerreso
War of Hearts - Ruelle
Hold Me Down - Halsey
Cry - Lena Fayre
Breathe - of Verona
Wicked Games - RAIGN

# STEALING AMY (DISCIPLES 2)

CHAPTER ONE

ANDREW

*Thump.*
"I simply don't understand it, Bart. You had everything in the palm of your hand…"

*Thump.*

My fist connects again with his body and this time it elicits a muffled screech. That tends to happen when someone's kidneys have been hit hard enough. It's strange, for such vital organs, the body sure didn't keep them hidden inside somewhere safe.

The screams and screeches peter out until I slam my fist against the other kidney. If I was a gambling man, which I'm not, I would say that Bart would be pissing blood for a week if he wasn't destined to die pretty soon.

"You were a part of the inner circle. You had your mouth

on the golden teat! How the fuck could you betray Lucifer?" I ask.

Standing in front of Bart, I shake my head at him. His eyes are wide with terror, and if I'm not mistaken, he pissed himself recently.

"All you had to do was tell Lucifer the Japs had approached you. You could have told him they were trying to pay you off. You know for a fact he would have fixed you up. He always takes care of us!"

I don't mean to scream that at the end, but Bart has to have known that.

Loyalties have been tested in the past with some of the guys, and every time Lucifer was there to make sure we followed him. To make sure we knew he was as loyal to us as we are to him.

The shrill sound of my phone ringing from my suit pocket stops me from swinging at his eyes. My fist is inches away from his nose when I stop myself.

I grin at him.

Wagging a finger in his eyes, I say, "Not just yet, be right back. You just hang out for me."

I pull the phone out of the suit jacket I left hanging on the back of the shitty chair in this room. Everything in this shitty room is fucking way past its prime. Then again, if it wasn't an abandoned old motel out in the middle of nowhere it wouldn't be so shitty.

"This is Andrew."

"Andrew, my friend!"

"Harrold, I was going to call you soon… How're things going?"

"Busy, as you well know. Mr. Lucifer informed me you would be needing my services today. I wanted to see if you had a time frame…"

Winking at a terrified Bart, I say, "Can you meet me at the old motel in about an hour? I won't be here much longer."

"I will be there."

"Thanks."

Disconnecting the phone, I put it back in my pocket before I pull the forty-five pistol from my shoulder holster. Bart is shaking now, and that wet spot I saw earlier is growing larger by the second.

The distinct smell of shit erupts in the air as I walk up to Bart and push the barrel of the pistol against his stomach.

"It's a shitty thing to know exactly how much more time you have left to live. To know you can't change the certainty of your own death."

Lowering the pistol towards his crotch, I pull the trigger.

The loud eruption of the gun in this small but tattered room deafens me. It's a few moments before I'm able to hear his loud screams through the ball gag I have crammed in his mouth.

"You're going to the afterlife a cockless bastard!" I roar over his screaming.

Aiming at his knee caps, I pull the trigger twice in rapid succession.

One in each knee cap.

The screaming continues for a few seconds before he passes out, his head slumping forward. Pain has a way of breaking everyone. He's no different than any other pile of shit out there.

Not any more he isn't.

Fucking little bitch is now one of the commoners. One of the fucking sheep out in the fucking herd that gets to die when the big bad fucking wolves tear his throat out.

There's a code in this world, it's an oath to each other that binds us. It's there to make sure we have each other's back, no matter what.

What he did... It's just not done.

We are all hard, battle-tested men who want the most from our role in life. He just threatened that role. He removed himself from being above the common crowd and put himself down in the mud like the rest of the fucking pigs.

Rolling in filth and shit.

Sitting in the chair that my coat hangs on is the small black leather bag I brought into this shitty motel with me. It's a fucking dump here, and I pray that I don't get bugs from the shitty room.

Pulling a hypodermic needle out of the bag, I take the bottle of adrenaline out as well. I fill the syringe as I walk over to Bart.

Back when I was in the SEALs, I served as a medic. Normally, I would never pull someone from a blackout like this…. it fucks with the body and will probably hurt his heart and brain pretty bad.

But he doesn't need to worry about those things.

I inject directly into the heart. His head snaps forward in wide-eyed misery as he comes back to reality.

Walking back to the bag, I pull out a small bottle of morphine.

His hands are stretched high above his head and he hangs from the ceiling supports. It doesn't help with injecting the pain meds.

Shrugging my shoulders, I push the medicine into a vein throbbing on the left side of his neck.

The drugs must work pretty damn well because his eyes lose that pain-filled haze and slowly begin to focus on me. I didn't give him much though, just enough to dull the pain but not cloud the mind.

"Bart, I know you were one of us so I won't send you to be fed to the pigs while you are alive. You get that much out of me. But Lucifer has a reputation to protect and so do I. I'm going to use you as a message to the Japs. You won't be alive to give it to them, but I'm pretty sure they will understand it all the same."

Pulling a scalpel from the bag, I first slice off his right ear then his left.

The screams are audible through the gag again and I'm tempted to do this after he dies, but I don't think that would be the right thing. He betrayed Lucifer and put the wife and kids in jeopardy—that can't be allowed *ever*.

But more importantly, he betrayed me and the men who serve our boss.

Taking out my anger again, I punch him in the mouth. I wince. Fuck, I think I hurt a knuckle with his teeth.

Shit, it's time to finish this off. I need a cold beer and a very hot pussy after shit like this.

He passes out sometime after I stab his eyes out.

No sight, no hearing, and no talking. He will go to them as a good message of what is to come for daring to attack us. To dare attack our boss.

Slicing the rope that is holding him up, his body falls to the ground in an almost boneless fashion. He's in the land of twilight now, not dead but almost.

I've never removed a tongue before and it makes my stomach quiver a bit.

My phone rings as I am unzipping my pants, my thick flaccid cock coming out of my boxers. "Fuck"

Walking over to my coat, I pull the phone out and walk back to the still-breathing body. I push connect at the exact moment I release a torrent of piss down on the bastard's face.

"Yeah?"

"We're here, Andrew."

"Ah, okay. Come on back, I'm done here."

My bladder comes to a stop as I finally empty it

completely. Bart's face turns towards me and he makes a loud, pitiful groan.

Kneeling down beside him, I say, "I hope you find even more torment in hell."

Putting the pistol to his forehead, I pull the trigger, and again the roar of the gun is deafening to my ears.

∽

CHAPTER TWO

AMY

ONE YEAR LATER

Ivan's baby blue eyes flick towards me, full of apology, as he focuses most of his attention on the phone pressed against his ear.

My eyes meet his and I keep expecting to feel *something*. To feel something more than this coldness that seeps inside of me.

Whoever he's listening to must say something to make him angry because his eyes narrow, no longer focusing on me, and he speaks sharply in Russian.

Honestly, I don't care that he has a phone call. Anything that pulls his attention away from me is a welcome relief.

I just want this stupid date to be over with.

Glancing down at my salad, I stab a piece of romaine lettuce a little more forcibly than required and push it into my mouth, chewing thoughtfully.

Ivan continues to speak rapidly in Russian and I don't understand a word he's saying except for the name *Lucifer*.

I never considered Ivan the religious type. In fact, I'm pretty sure the guy is a ruthless, heartless criminal who would sell his own mother if given half a chance. But more and more often lately, I keep hearing that name.

Has Ivan suddenly taken up faith?

It doesn't seem likely. Something else must be going on... Something that is pissing Ivan off.

Dropping my fork, I push my plate away and pick up my glass of wine. Slowly, my eyes glide over the room, taking in the upscale restaurant he brought me to. The décor is exquisite. Everything is done in white, gold, and sparkling crystal.

The clientele is impeccable; we're surrounded by the crème de la crème of Garden City. I recognize the mayor, a few A-list actors, and a rising pop star.

Everyone is dressed like they're ready to hit the red carpet or something—including the man sitting across from me.

Ivan looks like he just stepped off the cover of a magazine in his dark charcoal gray suit and blue silk tie. His suit jacket is unbuttoned, and he leans back in his chair. He is easily the most attractive man in the room, and it's done effortlessly.

He's beautiful, one of the most beautiful men I've ever laid eyes on with his short, white blonde hair, and baby blue eyes. His bone structure is flawless. Sharp cheekbones, a straight nose, and soft, kissable lips.

But his beauty does nothing but leave me feeling empty. No matter how hard I try to connect with him the connection just isn't there.

Sipping my wine, I know I should be flattered that a man like him is interested in a girl like me. And in the beginning, I was flattered... but no longer.

I've glimpsed the monster behind the beautiful mask and now I can't unsee it.

Two shadows move behind Ivan and I drink deeper.

I'm totally fucked and I don't know how to get myself out of this mess. Those two shadows are guarding Ivan's back, and I know there are at least two more at each exit. I could try to slip away, but even if I do succeed, what about Abigail?

My heart starts to race and I quickly have to shut down my panic. Freaking out will only make this worse.

So what if I don't have an excuse tonight to keep him out of my bed? Maybe it won't even come to that...

Ivan's rapid Russian slows and his blue eyes focus once more on me. He watches me drain the remaining wine in my glass and makes a motion with his hand. A waiter lingering beside the table rushes forward, refilling my glass before I even get it back down to the table.

Ivan's soft lips spread into a pleased smile and he picks up his glass of vodka, cheering me before tipping it back.

His eyes never leave my face as he drinks, and I know he expects me to join him. I also know that if I refuse the invitation that it will most likely make him angry... so I pick up my glass and tip it back.

Ivan drains his glass and the waiter steps forward to refill it but Ivan waves him away. I finish off half of my glass, feeling the warm buzz of alcohol warming my belly before I set it down on the table gently.

Ivan motions for the waiter to refill my glass for me.

Clenching my teeth together, I watch the waiter top my glass off and my cheeks burn with heat.

So it's come to this? He's resorting to getting me drunk so he can finally sleep with me...

Lifting my glass, I drain down the wine, drinking deeply. I need the alcohol's false courage to fortify me so I can make it through this night.

Ivan smirks and his eyes warm as he watches me.

He's been trying to sleep with me for weeks now, and I'm

not sure how I'm going to blow him off tonight. I'm running out of excuses.

How did my life come to this? Dreading the affections of such a man...

I bet half the women in this room would probably give their left tit to sleep with him.

They can have them if they want him.

I fucking hate him.

Eight weeks ago, Ivan walked into my life, and I wish he would have walked right back out of it. He walked into my work, a little clothing boutique downtown, looking for a present for his sister. Shamelessly, he flirted with me the entire time I helped him pick out a scarf. And given that he's so damn handsome, I was immediately taken with him.

I was over the moon when he returned the next week, and the week after that.

When he asked me out on a date, it was like a dream come true.

He's rich, beautiful, and powerful. And for those first couple of weeks, I wondered if I had somehow stepped into a fairy tale. He lavished me with expensive gifts and took me out to expensive restaurants. He even gifted me an entire new designer wardrobe.

But after a while, it was becoming very apparent that he expected me to repay him for the favors.

That was when the illusion started to fade for me. I began to notice his perfection was flawed. All the little things became more apparent. Still, I tried to return his affection, up to a point, but he always wanted more.

He demanded it.

I tried to break things off. I even attempted to return everything he ever gifted me, but he's a man who refuses to accept the word *no*.

After the first night I refused him, I started to notice

strange men following me to work. They'd linger outside the boutique during my shift, keeping tabs on me and everyone I interacted with.

At night, Ivan would show up at my door, questioning me about my day, and becoming more and more obsessive. I became afraid, and even looked into a restraining order, but all that did was piss him off and show me just how powerful he truly is…

Ivan speaks a few clipped words into his phone and then hangs up. Tucking the phone into his pocket, he leans forward and grabs my hand.

I resist the urge to pull my hand away. Something about his touch makes my skin crawl.

"My apologies, *myshka*," he purrs, fingers wrapping around me tightly. "But that was a very important call."

I nod my head and set my empty glass down on the table. Ivan nods towards the glass and the waiter steps forward, refilling it once more.

Ivan pulls my hand towards him and then lifts it to his mouth, lips tenderly brushing across my knuckles.

For a moment, I wonder what is wrong with me. Something inside of me must be broken. This beautiful man is bestowing his affections upon me but I find his touch repulsive. No matter how hard I try, I can't bring myself to enjoy it.

Neither his beauty nor his money can make up for all his horrible faults.

He's controlling, and aggressive when he gets angry. He hurt me the last time I refused to let him through my apartment door. He shoved me into the damn wall and pulled out a chunk of my hair in front of my daughter Abigail.

I'm trapped. The best I can do right now is try to make him happy so he doesn't kill me…

I try to pull my hand away from Ivan's mouth and his fingers tighten around me, squeezing painfully.

I endure the compression for as long as I can before a yelp slips past my lips.

Ivan's eyes flash and then he grins as if I've somehow pleased him. His grip relaxes and I let my hand drop to the table before trying to pull it back.

I watch him warily until I have my hand safely in my own lap.

Leaning back, he flicks his fingers at his empty glass and his vodka is refilled immediately.

"Amy..." he purrs huskily.

Rubbing my hand beneath the table cloth, I make my expression as neutral as possible. "Yes?"

"Finish your drink."

Inside, I'm fuming. Reaching out, I grab my drink and it takes every ounce of self-control I have to keep from tossing it in his smirking face. He lifts his own glass and sips from it while watching me.

I bring my glass to my mouth and my stomach twists as I sip. Already, the wine is sour on my tongue and the warm buzz has become an annoying after-effect.

Our eyes meet over the rims of our glasses. His bore into mine like icy daggers until I finish the wine off completely. The glass empty, I'm afraid to set it back down on the table, afraid he'll order the waiter to refill it.

I lean back, keeping the empty glass in my grip.

Smirk sharpening, Ivan snaps his fingers and a body peels away from the shadows, one of his beefy bodyguards coming forward. Murmured words are exchanged between the two before a long, black velvet box is produced.

My eyes fall upon the box and I'm filled with dread and trepidation. Another gift? Please no...

Setting his glass down on the table, Ivan rises and approaches me, the box in his hand.

Watching him approach, I shake my head. "Ivan... You shouldn't have..."

Seriously, he shouldn't have. Every gift he's ever given me he's used to force some kind of repayment out of me. In the beginning it was sweet, he would only ask for another date.

More recently though it's become a kiss while his hands try to fondle me...

He plucks the empty glass from my hand and sets it on the table. Immediately the waiter comes forward and refills it.

"Ah, but I must, my *myshka*. Tonight is a special night, and I want you to remember it always."

Bending over me, he snaps the box open in front of my eyes. I blink at all the diamonds, their dazzling sparkles almost blinding me.

"It's too much... I can't possibly accept it," I protest softly as he lifts the strands of diamonds from the box.

Ivan clicks his tongue against the roof of his mouth as he wraps the strands around my neck. "It's only a trinket."

"A trinket?" I repeat incredulously. The three strands are completely covered in diamonds, and I know they must be worth thousands.

"Yes," he says, his breath tickling my ear. "Only a trinket. When you give me my heir then I will present you with proper jewels."

Heir? What the fuck? This is the first I'm hearing of this...

Ivan buries his face in my hair and breathes in deep.

I shudder, wanting to rip the diamonds off of my neck.

"Come," he says, pulling away and grabbing me by my sore hand.

"Where are we going?" I ask, trying not to panic as he pulls me to my feet.

His arm wraps around my waist, bringing me close. "It's time to retire for the evening."

I shake my head and glance around, searching for an escape.

My eyes fall upon the table. "But I didn't even get to finish my drink…"

Ivan tips his head back, chuckling. Reaching around me, he grabs my glass and hands it to me. "Here, you can finish on the way."

Pushing the glass into my hand, I have no choice but to accept it. He gives me a pointed look until I lift the glass to my lips and drink.

Fuck it. If I have to endure this, I might as well be drunk.

Neck arching back, I drain the wine completely as he guides me. His fingers flex around my hip protectively and he leads me to the back of the restaurant, through the kitchen, and to a door that opens to the back alley.

He has some silly rule about never leaving through the front.

I set the empty glass on a counter before we pass through the back door, stepping into the night. Ivan's black limo is idling and the chauffeur holds the back door open for us.

Ivan pauses for a moment, looking towards the two bodyguards in the alley before dragging me forward. We take three steps and then Ivan tenses beside me.

Dropping my hand, he whirls around, and everything happens so fast I'm not sure what is happening.

Ivan crumbles to the ground and one of his bodyguards approaches me.

For a hysterical moment, I want to thank the bodyguard for knocking out Ivan but then the man grabs me. His hand slaps over my mouth and my lips are stuck together, I can't move them.

I gaze up at the bodyguard, my eyes wide and watering as I scream behind the tape in panic.

His face hardens and then the world goes black.

As the black silk hood settles over my head and two strong arms lift me up, I can't help but feel a little relieved…

How fucked up is that?

CHAPTER THREE

ANDREW

Bagged and gagged. That went almost too easy, but for now, I'm not going to complain. Shit, I even have a hot fucking chick in the back with our package, but it's going to be a shame if I have to consider her excess baggage.

Lucifer doesn't like baggage when it comes to jobs. He wants everything neat and orderly. And this is a whopper of excess baggage.

We were supposed to take only Ivan and the wife, not his bimbo.

Snagging his fuck-toy was a must though when he brought the girl out the back door with him. If he hadn't been such a gigantic douche nozzle, manhandling her out the door like he did, we could have snatched him and left her in the dust.

Shit. Things like this only lead to fucking complications. I don't want complications. Fuck, it should have been his stupid fucking wife. Not this… this… fucking sexy young girl.

Shaking my head, I frown at the two people sitting across from me in the black limousine.

Turning my head, I tell Peter, "Let's get to the warehouse,

but add a few minutes to the trip. I need to figure out what to do about our little complication."

Peter nods his head and I turn back to watch my prisoners for a few more minutes. The girl is sitting there, stiff as a board. Her every muscle looks locked in strain as she turns her head towards every little sound.

I bet she's coming to grips with her dire situation. I bet she knows she is a loose strand, like a weed that needs to be plucked from the garden.

I fucking hate killing women, it turns my stomach when I do it, but… Fuck. Stupid fucking Ivan is dooming her.

Leaning forward, I growl out, "You stupid fuck, Ivan."

Lashing out with a fist, I snap it into the bag that's hiding that shit-fuck's face. I feel the protruding bulge of his nose before the sharp stab of pain lances through my hand.

The scream of pain from behind his gag is just a little louder than my growl of, "Fuck!"

Shaking my hand, I hear a chuckle coming from the front seat behind me. I've fucked my damn hand up again. This damn hand has been nagging me all year.

Peter says, "Shit, did you just fuck your hand up again, Andrew?"

Ignoring him, I reach forward and whip the bag off of Ivan's head.

He's got fucking spirit though, I'll give him that. Bloody nose, tears streaking down his cheeks. He still looks pissed off. And if looks could kill? I'd be castrated.

Shaking my hand, I rub the knuckle that is sending sharp stabs of pain through it. I fractured the damn thing when I was taking care of Bart, and I haven't really had a chance to let the thing heal up.

Too many people are getting swept up into the maelstrom that is Lucifer's rage. It's been a year of fire and brimstone.

Too bad Ivan's on the wrong side of the fence right now.

I'm positive he's never been on the receiving end of the treatment he's getting right now. Well, fuck him and his bitch ass looks. Dude isn't going to be such a pretty boy now.

That fucking broken nose will make sure of that.

"You've become a problem, Ivan. Now, usually Lucifer would handle things like you exclusively… But that's not how things are happening now. The inner circle has been unleashed on fucks like you."

He yells a bunch of words through the tape but they are too gargled to understand.

Shrugging my shoulders at him, I say, "Can't understand a single fucking word you're saying right now. I'd remove that tape from your mouth, but then you would probably be squealing like your bimbo over there."

Looking at her fully for a moment, I can appreciate what the man sees in this girl.

Her legs look fucking amazing. She wasn't put into the car gently, so the eyeful of legs and just a hint of exposed crotch is a pretty fucking hot sight.

She looks a little too elegant for someone like Ivan, too… She doesn't look fake like Ivan's wife does. No, this girl has never had the touch of a surgeon's knife.

From what I saw of her in the restaurant… fuck. If she was mine, I'd never let her out of my bed.

He screams at me again through the tape, and I can tell Ivan really doesn't appreciate me looking at his chick.

Fuck him.

Turning to look at him, I just can't take all the noise he keeps spurting out like some fucking stuck pig.

Leaning forward again, I slam my fist into his stomach. The air expels from his nose explosively and he loses all focus on me.

Turning my head to Peter, I say, "Take us to the warehouse. We'll see what Lucifer wants to do. We need this pile of shit out of the car. He smells like sour vodka and piss."


AMY

I can't see. No matter how much I blink my eyes, there's no light. No hint of anything around me. Only darkness.

This damn bag on my head is stifling.

At first, when I was grabbed and tossed into whatever vehicle we're in, I was on the verge of hyperventilating. Panicking about my situation. But I cut that shit out quick. All it got me was my own hot breath in my face and that totally sucked ass.

*Complication.* They haven't outright said it but I know that's me. Whatever they have planned, I'm not supposed to be a part of it.

Somewhere near me is a man, a man with a very deep, rumbling voice, who is holding my life in his hands.

If I could beg or plead, I would. I'd get down on my knees and promise anything. But all I can do is sit here on this seat and pray that they realize I'm no threat. I won't talk about anything that's happened.

They only want Ivan... and fuck, they can totally have him. Whatever they have planned for him he probably deserves it.

My lips are sealed.

I know it's useless trying to do anything about this.

You see, I've already learned my lesson when dealing with these kinds of men. They do the things they do and get it away with it because they're not afraid of the authorities. They are the authorities in Garden City. Meting out their own rules and justice.

They have the police and the judges and everyone else above them in their pockets.

I learned this the hard way when I tried to get a restraining order against Ivan. Not only was my petition dismissed, the judge actually lectured me about wasting his time and advised me to make up with Ivan. He threatened to turn the authorities on *me*.

Beside me Ivan gurgles and I strain my ears, trying to listen over him. The man who spoke earlier is quiet now. Too quiet.

If only I could speak. If only I could say something...

I can sense him though. I can feel his eyes boring into me. All the little hairs on my body stand on end, pointing towards him.

I'm terrified of him, yet something about that fear also excites me.

I feel so fucked up for feeling like this.

The vehicle slows and comes to a complete stop. The engine turns off.

Fuck, this is it.

One of the doors opens, and I feel a burst of cold air hitting my legs. Ivan grunts and I sense a struggle beside me.

"Fuck, he does stink," someone mutters unhappily. "Come on, you stupid fuck."

The air beside me moves and then there's a thump. A body hitting the pavement?

"Really? You're going to make me drag you?"

There's a series of grunts and the gritty sound of gravel grinding against something.

I'm so focused on what's going on outside that I completely forget about the danger inside.

Suddenly a warm hand comes down on my bare thigh and I gasp, stiffening.

Strong fingers wrap around my thigh, digging into my flesh. But the grip doesn't hurt... No, there's something about it that's strangely possessive.

The fingers relax, flexing, and then they drag upwards. "You're going to be a good girl, yes?" the deep voice asks.

For a heartbeat I'm so terrified I do nothing. Then quickly realizing my mistake, I start to rapidly nod my head.

*I'll be a good girl. I'll be so good*, I try to mentally project to him.

I'll do anything to make it home to Abigail.

His hand reaches the apex of my thigh and then there's a pressure. Oh god... Does he want me to spread for him?

"If you do everything you're told," he growls and pushes harder, forcing me to open my legs for him. "I just might be able to get you out of this."

Might?! He *might* be able to get me out of this?

Once again I start to pant, my own hot little breaths hitting the bag.

His fingers move and then I feel them brushing against my panties. I freeze.

"Would be such a shame..." he mutters and then his hand pulls away.

The tension breaks and my lungs pull in much needed air. Before I can think too much about what he just said, or did for that matter, my arm is grabbed and I'm pulled out of the vehicle.

Stumbling, I try to get my bearings.

The cool air hits me and I shiver, straightening. Fingers tighten around my arm, pulling me forward.

My heels dig into gravel and I'm grateful for the firm grip that guides me. The small rocks cause me to slip and slide a bit.

More than a couple of times I almost fall on my ass.

After a few minutes, we step inside a building, shielded from the biting wind.

No longer focusing all of my attention on trying to

prevent a twisted ankle, I realize there was a conversation going on that just ended abruptly.

Because of me?

All at once my hackles rise and my chest constricts with panic.

I can't see them but I can feel them. The monsters in the darkness…

A door slams behind me and I nearly jump out of my skin.

The grip around my arm tightens, nudging me forward, then digs in deep when I don't budge.

I'm too frightened to keep moving.

My heels are trying to dig into the smooth floor while alarm bells go off inside my head.

"Be a good girl," the deep voice from earlier hisses as he drags me forward.

I'm already fucking up, I quickly realize. How the hell am I going to make it through this?

The fingers around my arm loosen and then I'm pushed backward, stumbling before I land on a chair.

Rattled, I shake my head a little and then my arms are yanked behind my back. My wrists slam together, and something is wrapped around them. Tightly binding them.

It all happens so quick, it's so damn efficient… they must have a lot of practice at this…

Beside me, someone groans in agony and it takes me a moment to realize it's Ivan.

Suddenly, the bag is yanked off my head and my eyes blur with tears as they adjust to the bright spotlight beaming down on me. I blink quickly to clear them.

Standing in front of me, with a smirk tugging at his lips, is the most beautiful man I've ever laid eyes on.

He's so beautiful, so unreal and ethereal, at first I think he must be a figment of my imagination. Blonde hair and blue eyes. Features so perfect I can find no flaw in them. The light seems to caress his glowing skin, but the longer and longer I look at him, the more I feel distressed.

He's too perfect… almost angelic.

But no angel would be in a place like this.

My eyes start to shy away from the beautiful man but then he steps forward, grabs a lock of my hair, and lifts it.

The smirk on his lips sharpens and he glances to my left.

I look over and gasp behind the tape covering my mouth. Ivan has been tied to a chair beside me, but his face is messed up. His right eye is swollen closed and his nose looks broken, bent crooked. And there's dried blood caking his nostrils and the tape covering his mouth.

"I could have sworn your wife was a blonde, Ivan," the beautiful man says with some amusement as his fingers rub my hair thoughtfully before dropping it.

Wife? Ivan is married?

You've got to be fucking kidding me…

My eyes narrow angrily at Ivan and the beautiful man tips his head back and laughs.

I ignore him, my anger momentarily overriding my good sense as his words repeat inside of my head.

All this time. All this *fucking* time Ivan has been pursuing me—stalking me and trying to control me—he's been married?!

Buying me things… Taking me out… Trying to sleep with me… When he already has a wife at home?

And he never mentioned it. No, I would have remembered that. I would have ended it immediately.

I wouldn't even be in this mess.

Fuck.

He's made me the other woman.

My stomach twists painfully and I feel like getting sick.

Laughter dying away, the beautiful man in front of me

takes a step toward Ivan and reaches out, ripping the tape off that covers Ivan's mouth in one swift movement.

Ivan groans and I wince. That looked incredibly painful, especially with all the dried blood that came off with the tape.

"Well?" our captor says with a bit of disgust, dropping the tape to the floor. "Do you have anything to say for yourself, Ivan?"

Ivan eyes our captor warily and then slowly shakes his head.

"Are you sure?" the beautiful man presses. "You don't even want to know why I've brought you here?"

Ivan takes in a breath, licks his bloodied lips, and then his eyes flick to me. "Why have you brought me here, Lucifer?"

Lucifer? This is the same Lucifer I hear Ivan talking about so often?

Lucifer grins and says with some satisfaction, "Well, with everything I've been hearing through the pipelines, I figured you had something you wanted to tell me."

Taking in Ivan's pale face and compressed lips, Lucifer scowls. "No? I was mistaken?"

Ivan's eyes dart around the room with a hint of desperation as if he's looking for an exit or way to escape this. I feel my own panic growing inside of my chest even though I don't really understand what's happening.

"Ah, well, if you have nothing to say, Ivan, I guess this was all just a waste of our time..."

Lucifer turns towards me and for a brief, glorious moment I truly believe this has all been a big misunderstanding and he's going to release me.

Then he reaches down, pulls a gun from his hip and presses it against my forehead.

The blood in my veins freezes and my heart stops beating.

I can't move, breathe, or blink.

I'm going to die. This beautiful man is going to blow my brains all over the concrete.

Thanks to Ivan, I'll never see my daughter again.

The weight of my life hanging in the balance is more than my mind can process. My thoughts race but everything around me begins to move in slow motion.

"No!" Ivan bellows and I watch the shadows behind Lucifer separate. A man steps forward, forming out of the darkness.

"No?" Lucifer repeats, sounding confused as he glances towards Ivan.

I can't look towards Ivan, my eyes are locked on the dark newcomer, drawn to him like a magnet. He takes a step forward, into the light, and for a hysterical second, I wonder if he means to save me as his hand drops to his hip.

But then his features come more into focus, and any hope I held withers inside of my heart.

The man looks so mean, so angry, his black eyes smoldering with such intense hatred as he glares at me, I realize he's probably just one of Lucifer's goons. Ready to back him up and shoot me dead if I somehow manage to escape the gun pressed against my head.

I hear Ivan clear his throat and say, "Perhaps there was something I wished to discuss with you..."

"Perhaps?" Lucifer repeats, incredulous. The barrel of the gun presses harder against my forehead and I whimper as it digs into my skin. "I don't have time for this shit..."

Lucifer's finger begins to move over the trigger and I squeeze my eyes shut, hoping it's quick.

"No! Wait!" Ivan cries out again. "There are many things I would like to discuss with you. Just don't hurt her..."

"What things?" Lucifer drawls out, sounding like he doesn't believe Ivan.

"Things regarding some mutual acquaintances of ours… from Japan.

I feel the gun pull away and my eyes pop open.

Lucifer's lips quirk up into a smirk and I see something flashing across his eyes. Satisfaction with a hint of amusement?

"Go on," he prompts Ivan.

There's a heavy pause and I watch Lucifer stiffen with irritation. He begins to lift the gun again, and my nose tingles painfully while spots dance in front of my eyes.

I don't know how much more I can take of this before I die of a heart attack.

"I want assurances that you won't kill me… or my mistress…"

"You're in no position to bargain."

"I know the person directly responsible for ordering the hit on your wife."

Lucifer laughs. "You do, do you?"

"Yes," Ivan says quickly. "I also know that there's to be another hit soon, on your children…"

The room, cold and silent up until now, feels like it explodes with a flurry of whispers and movements.

"Keep talking," Lucifer growls angrily. The gun drops away as he forgets about me and focuses all of his attention on Ivan.

"Only if you agree to my terms…" Ivan stammers.

Lucifer stiffens then his head turns towards me. His eyes, so bright, so cold now, I feel the full force of his anger and loathing.

If I were a bug, he would stomp me out of existence.

"Andrew," he snaps, and the man that formed in the shadows takes another step forward, into the light.

"Yes, sir?"

"Get rid of her," Lucifer orders and turns away.

Oh my god, he's not even going to do it himself. He just ordered his goon to kill me...

Eyes as black as a moonless night, the one Lucifer called Andrew glares murderously at me as he begins to approach me.

He's so big.

He's freakin' massive, I realize as he grows wider and taller, his feet eating up the distance between us.

Perhaps tonight has been just too much. My mind has cracked. Something inside of me must be broken. Because I swear that even though Andrew is in the light now, the shadows from the corner have traveled with him.

And as he stops in front of me, reaching for me, those shadows wrap around me, seeping into my skin.

Vaguely, my brain registers four words, "Be a good girl," before my eyes roll into the back of my head.

Purchase Stealing Amy on Amazon to continue reading...

ALSO BY IZZY AND SEAN

**Disciples**

Keeping Lily (Lily & Lucifer)

Stealing Amy (Amy & Andrew)

**The Pounding Hearts Series**

Banging Reaper (Chase & Avery)

Slamming Demon (Brett & Mandy)

Bucking Bear (Max & Grace)

Breaking Beast (Alex & Christy)

BY SARA PAGE & SEAN MORIARTY

**Star Joined**

Craving Maul

**By Sean Moriarty**

Gettin' Lucky

Gettin' Dirty

**By Izzy Sweet**

Letting Him In

Stepbrother Catfish

Printed in Great Britain
by Amazon